GUN GAMES

A Novella

J BARTELL

&

GINGER MARIN

DEDICATION

*Dedicated to the indomitable spirit of those who, in the face of
overwhelming adversity, find the courage to stand for justice.
And to the belief that even in our darkest hours,
there is a light of hope that can ignite change.*

CONTENTS

CONTENTS

CHAPTER ONE
GAMESMANSHIP

The thumping bass and aggressive lyrics of gangsta rap reverberated through the night of a Los Angeles neighborhood.

A gleaming black Charger with a custom *Day of the Dead* skull, emblazoned across the bottom of the driver's side door, rolled down the street with silver rims and neon underglow. The windows were tinted. In the backseat, Naldo, 30s, sharp-eyed and dangerously high-strung, the fierce mastermind. He leaned forward, his jittering leg betraying an undercurrent of tension. Perez, late 20s, the eager driver with a hustler's energy, kept his eyes on the road, taking every turn with precision. Riding shotgun was Big Frankie, a human battering ram in his 30s, his bulk making the car's frame groan under the strain. The men were all dressed in fitted dark cargo pants, designer hoodies, chunky gold chains, and bandanas in their purple and gold gang colors.

The car eased up to a darkened street corner where three drug dealers loitered under a dim, flickering streetlamp, their conversations halting as the vehicle approached. Without hesitation, the gangbangers spilled out in a blur of movement, sending two of the dealers stumbling back instinctively. Naldo's hand was tight around his gun.

Naldo nodded sharply to Big Frankie, who wasted no time. He circled behind the remaining dealer, a wiry man rooted in place by fear, and yanked him to his knees. Big Frankie tore the man's bandana from his head and stuffed it deep into his mouth. Meanwhile, Perez kept a watchful eye on the other two dealers, who were visibly cowering in fear.

Hovering over the captive, Naldo brandished his nine millimeter, the barrel catching the dim light. His voice, low and steady, dripped with menace. "You think you can move merch without us knowing?"

The words barely had time to register before Naldo struck. The first blow landed hard, the butt of the gun crunching against the man's ear. He grunted, collapsing onto his hands, but Big Frankie hauled him back up, holding him in place for the next strike. By the time Naldo finished, the man's ear dangled by a thread of cartilage, blood pooling at his feet.

The other two dealers stood frozen, wide-eyed and too terrified to move. At Perez' abrupt motion, they emptied their pockets, turning them inside out to reveal paltry sums. Perez sneered, his disgust palpable. The downed dealer, finally grasping the futility of resistance, fumbled through his pockets and produced wads of crumpled bills — fives, tens, and twenties. Frankie scooped them up and handed them to Naldo, who pocketed them without so much as a glance.

But the bangers weren't satisfied yet. Naldo wanted to make a point. He delivered a brutal kick to the dealer's face. The force sent what remained of the man's ear flying into the gutter. As the gangbangers got back into the car, its tires rolled over the ear, crushing it into the asphalt along with the cheap, fake diamond embedded in the lobe.

The next morning, across town, Councilman Javier Rico was in a race against time. At 40, he was a sharp, charismatic advocate for the people, his gritty determination honed by years as a Marine. At the moment, though, he was furiously searching his office for a critical document while tuning in to a live stream of the city council meeting. The echoes of heated arguments and frustrated pleas filled the city council chambers. The voices clashed and overlapped, creating a cacophony of conflicting opinions and agendas, bureaucracy and ego.

"Just table S449 until the next session!" one councilman's voice rang out through the speakers.

Rico's heart sank as he shuffled through a stack of papers. He moved faster.

His desk bore signs of a life driven by purpose: framed photos of his wife and daughter, side-by-side images of him in battle gear, his Marine unit frozen in time on foreign soil. A standout photo featured his hands resting protectively on the shoulders of two Afghan children clutching books. The walls were adorned with medals and more pictures of his military service, each one representing a physical mark of his sacrifices.

"No way! Keep that up and the only kids left alive will be the gangs," shouted a voice from the public gallery, its plea raw with urgency.

"She's right. We can't keep putting this off," he heard one of the councilwomen say.

"Do something now for Christ's sake!" came another plea from a member of the audience. "Our kids are dying because of you!"

Rico finally located the document and bolted for the chamber.

Inside, the dais stretched before him, lined with 15 council members — a cross-section of Los Angeles' diversity, their faces ranging from hardened indifference to earnest concern. Voices overlapped from every corner of the room, the gallery still hot with outrage.

As Rico entered, applause erupted — not for him, but in response to a passionate outburst from the gallery.

"Fine," said the first councilman, "we'll talk about it. People want guns off the streets now, not more church socials."

Rico couldn't hold back. "You're equating getting young people jobs with church socials?!"

"They don't want jobs, not if they can make more money selling drugs."

"Then let's start with better incentives and tax credits to businesses so we can increase the minimum wage," said Rico. "And I think my bill S449 can accomplish that and more." He waved his amended document then passed copies of it down the dais.

Councilwoman Maya Park, a Korean American in her late 30s and a firm supporter of Rico's efforts, smiled at him at the same time the first councilman came back with, "You're forgetting the cuts needed to balance the budget."

"I'm not forgetting," Rico shot back, his tone sharp enough to silence murmurs in the gallery. "But instead of cutting social programs, let's take an ax to our own bloated salaries, pensions, and benefits. If we want to balance the budget, let's start right here!"

The chamber erupted in scattered applause from the public. Councilwoman Park chuckled softly, watching the first councilman squirm. "I support S449," Park announced firmly.

The rest of the council exchanged uneasy glances and murmured their disapproval. Just as Rico opened his mouth to press further, the chamber doors burst open.

Mr. Kim's voice rang out first. "They robbed and shot up my grocery store again!" He was trembling with frustration. "You said you'd do something!" The Kim family flooded in behind him, Mrs. Kim leading the way, flanked by their three children, aged 10 to 17, and a young Latino employee.

Several council members immediately called for security, their voices overlapping in disarray.

"Great," Rico muttered, his expression hardening. "Here's a hardworking businessman, and you treat *him* like the threat."

"People can't just barge in here—"

"Shut up and let them speak!" Councilwoman Park snapped, her sharp tone cutting through the chaos.

The Kims' young employee stepped forward, his voice steady despite the tension. "If the Kims shut down, I lose my job. How do I pay for school?"

The first councilman rose to leave, but Mrs. Kim stepped forward, holding up a package of diapers riddled with bullet holes. "You want to ignore us?" she said, her voice thick with emotion. "This is what we live with every day!"

The room fell silent as the councilmen exchanged uneasy looks. Slowly, they sat back down.

As the meeting ended in chaos, Rico and Park walked side by side toward the elevators.

"I thought Beatty was going to choke when you mentioned salaries. I swear, everything about that man is bloated. Seriously,

Javier, have you thought more about running for Mayor. I think it's your time."

"Wouldn't know it from that meeting."

As they reached the elevator, Mr. Kim, being escorted out with his family, caught Rico's eye. The faintest smile flickered across his face — a shared moment of gratitude and understanding. "Well played," Park murmured as the elevator doors opened. "For all of them."

Afterwards, they each went back to their respective offices to take on the rest of the day's agenda. For Park, it was answering constituent mail. For Rico, it was back to scouring his bill S449 to make sure he addressed every single objection the council came up and even a few new ones he was now anticipating.

That night, the air was thick with the smell of gunpowder and the sound of excited chatter as a sport shooting exposition took place on the outskirts of Los Angeles.

It was situated in a large open field with tents and booths set up throughout. The main banner promoting the event — *"Jobs for Kids Charity Shoot Off — Sponsored by ShowGun"* — hung high above the entrance, its brightly colored letters standing out against the clear night sky.

The atmosphere was lively, with bursts of laughter and conversation mixed with cheerful country music playing from a nearby stage. The occasional gunshot could be heard from the shooting range positioned at the far end, with high earthen berms for safety, backing the targets.

The booths were adorned with flags and signs, some showcasing products like gun safes and accessories, and country-style furnishings, while others offered samples of specialty foods. Vendors called out to passersby, enticing them to come try their products. The smoky aroma of barbecue wafted through the air as families milled about, enjoying the spectacle. Some were dressed in camouflage gear; others wore country-style attire. Children ran around playing games and laughing as adults chatted and shopped.

Rico entered the grounds wearing jeans, sneakers and a black polo shirt with the logo "ShowGun" and carrying a shooting bag. He was accompanied by his lovely 24-year-old daughter Dolores — the one in the photo in Rico's office — radiating with youthful energy and pride, her lustrous hair catching the glow of the fair's lights.

A family from Rico's district ran up, their young son eagerly holding out a phone for a selfie. Rico obliged with a warm smile, while Dolores stepped aside to let them all enjoy the moment. "Good luck, Dad! See you after the match," she said.

The atmosphere was electric as the bleachers filled behind them, a sea of excited faces eagerly waiting for the charity shoot-off. A booming voice over the loudspeaker reminded everyone that the event was mere minutes away.

Rico strode confidently toward his team, a formidable group of ex-military and law enforcement professionals who were gathered in the preparation area. They were all dressed in matching black polo shirts, signaling their unity and readiness for the task at hand. Among them was Mair Carling, an athletic 30-year old stuntwoman with toned muscles and a determined look in her eyes. Bobby Lopez, in his late 20s, exuded confidence and charm as a member of L.A. SWAT. Mark Jamieson, 40, stood tall and imposing as Bobby's formidable SWAT leader.

Each one checked their equipment and conventional "service" type weapons with precision and ease. Rico shared a special bond with Mair, evident in the exchange of smiles between them as he pulled out his shooting gear from his bag. He swiftly put on his gunbelt and loaded his magazines, ready to face the challenges that lay ahead. The air was tense with anticipation and adrenaline as they geared up for action.

Across from them was the rival team, "Super Squad," exuding a sleek and polished look with their sponsored outfits and optical-enhanced weapons. Professional competition shooters aged between late 20s-40s.

A sports broadcaster entered the area with a microphone. "Mr. Councilman, how about a few words for the good people who came out to support your cause?" Members of both teams and spectators applauded and cheered.

"Thank you all for showing up and supporting this charity. It's heartwarming to see our community pulling together to help at-risk kids find jobs." As Rico spoke, Bobby spotted five gang members move in the crowd outside the shooting range. He left the prep area.

Rico continued, "I'd like to thank the owner of ShowGun, Mair Carling, and our friends from the L.A.P.D. for investing so much time into making this event a reality." Applause came from the crowd.

Along the concourse, though, Naldo walked with his crew. Bobby stepped in front of him. "You're outside your turf."

"Who are you to get in my face?" blustered Naldo.

"A concerned citizen," Bobby replied calmly.

Big Frankie leaned in and whispered something to Naldo.

"Oh, yeah, now I know you," Naldo sneered. "Why don't you go concern yourself with whatever the fuck you was doing. This is a public event."

Bobby stood his ground. "No gangs allowed."

Naldo scoffed. "You like to shoot. We like to shoot. What the fuck's the problem?" Then as if on cue, Naldo got right into Bobby's face. "You think you're better than us? All I gotta do is snap my fingers."

"What a cliché," Bobby retorted coolly.

"What did you call me?" Naldo seethed.

Naldo's men instantly surrounded Bobby but before the situation could escalate further, an authoritative voice cut through the tension. "Bobby, you're holding things up." It came from Morrison, a 40-year-old Black man who was especially big and intense looking. He was flanked by two other men as he stepped into the group.

"There isn't a problem here, is there boys?" Morrison asked calmly as he turned his baseball cap from backwards to forwards. The cap read U.S. Marines. The other two men followed suit and put on their caps, also representing the Marine Corps.

"Is there?" Bobby challenged Naldo.

Reluctantly, Naldo backed off with his crew. "Another time, esse," he spat out as they left. As the group of bangers dispersed, they flashed their gang hand signals to no one in particular, a silent warning of their presence and power.

"Fucking minorities," said Morrison. Team ShowGun and their companions chuckled as they walked away.

At the broadcasters' booth, two men sat overlooking the shooting ranges and began their commentary. "This is one for the books," said one. "Stock guns against the weapons elite. Iron sights against special optics."

As the broadcasters set up the action for the crowd, the teams entered the match ranges and took their places. "The rules are simple. The shooters will engage identical multi-colored targets. Super Squad on the left. Team ShowGun on the right. Four members on each team and both teams compete on identical setups, consisting of four separate shooting ranges. This is a relay-style event."

The second broadcaster continued. "First shooter runs to the firing line on the buzzer, draws, engages targets. When they holster, the next team member goes. Four shooters, four ranges, same setup for both teams."

The actual firing line was ten yards further downrange. A shooter from each team stepped up to the start line. "First up Bobby Lopez and Tony Bocelli," announced the second broadcaster.

A match official stood behind Bobby and Tony and commanded, "Shooters load up." The men efficiently loaded their weapons.

"Shooters ready?" Each of the shooters nodded.

"Stand by." A couple of seconds later, a buzzer sounded causing Bobby and Tony to run up to the firing line while carousel music began to play.

"Bobby's a member of the L.A.P.D. SWAT team and Tony placed second in this year's National Open championships."

Bobby and Tony had reached the firing line which caused a tarp further downrange to drop. A fun house facade with duplicate clown cutouts holding multi-colored balloons on strings appeared. A flashing sign told them to "Shoot Blue."

Bobby aimed and shot at his blue balloons. Tony's optical red dot was easily seen on his balloons. He fired, quickly hitting one after the other, then re-holstered.

"Tony has re-holstered, signaling his teammate to go."

Jennifer Williams, who was at the next range, took off running.

"Here come the ladies. Jennifer Williams first out, two time national champion in her class."

Bobby now hit his last balloon and re-holstered which sent Mair running.

"Here comes Mair Carling. She's a stuntwoman and weapons expert for the studios!"

A tarp dropped. Duplicate carnival test-your-strength-towers appeared with flashing signs "Shoot Green." The mallet was poised above with six multi-colored plates attached to the sides of the tower. Jennifer's red dot scope made it easy to hit the plates. Mair fired. Clean hits but slower than Jennifer whose last plate fell. Jennifer's tower bell rang and she re-holstered, sending teammate Franklin DeWitt running.

"Optics equals speed. I don't see how ShowGun has a chance to win. Next up, Champion Franklin DeWitt against Mark Jamieson whose day job is working for the Los Angeles Police Department."

When Franklin reached the firing line, a tarp dropped. This one revealed a big concession stand with a flashing sign "Shoot Red." Duplicate large multi-colored apples hung from a wire, moving left to right. Franklin fired and missed. It took him 3 to 4 shots to hit each apple.

"Ha! Will you look at that. He's losing the red dot of his scope against the red apples."

Jamieson finally arrived and rapidly obliterated his red apples.

"Looks like Team ShowGun's making some headway after all."

Jamieson hit his last apple and re-holstered which sent Rico running.

"Coming down to the finish line now, Councilman Javier Rico. And right behind him is Mason Smith, last year's World Champion."

Mason and Rico arrived at the firing line at the same time. The tarp dropped. Two water tanks, two laughing fat lady dummies in old-fashioned bathing suits atop diving boards anchored with ropes and hardware. The flashing sign read "Shoot Gold." There was a series of multi-colored door knobs.

"The Councilman will have a tough time here. These targets are tailor-made for optics."

Mason hit his first gold knob. His Fat Lady slid a little closer to the end of the diving board. Rico took longer to aim his iron sights. He made the shot just as Mason hit another knob. Mason's Fat Lady was now closer to the edge. As Rico aimed, he spotted a glint of metal from the rope's hardware holding up his Fat Lady's board. He stopped shooting.

"What the heck is he doing?"

Rico realigned his sights and fired multiple shots at the hardware. The bullets pinged against the metal and snapped. Rico's Fat Lady splashed into the tank, still laughing. Mason fired, his Fat Lady hit the water, a second too late.

The crowd went crazy.

"The Fat Lady ain't gonna sing no more! All right for the Councilman... but what exactly did he hit?"

Officials held up Rico's dummy and pointed at the brass hardware.

"It's gold!" the Match Official proclaimed.

"Well, I'll be. A coup for Team ShowGun. The rules said he had to hit what's colored gold. You have to give him credit."

At the end of the match, members of the elite Super Squad offered their congratulations to the ShowGun shooters. Handshakes and smiles were exchanged between the teams. ShowGun then proudly displayed a large cardboard check made out to "Jobs for Teens." Mair turned to Rico with a knowing look. "You always have something up your sleeve, eh?" He responded with a sly wink.

Dolores entered the area and pumped her arms in a congratulatory gesture. Mair spotted the sparkle of a diamond ring. "Oh my God, Dolores! Who? When?"

"You're all invited!"

Bobby also saw the ring. "Oh, wow, who's the lucky guy?"

Rico answered. "She's marrying the director of Flamenco de la Madrid, the best dance company in all of Spain."

"Olé," shouted Bobby.

"Now, let's eat. I'm starved," said Rico as he led the group toward the barbecue area. Mair huddled close to him. "How's it going downtown?" she asked, concerned.

"Oh, you know, no money, lousy schools, drugs... stupid kids killing each other."

"So, the usual?"

Rico smiled and shook his head wearily. "How's business with you?"

"The usual." She smiled back at him then turned her attention to Dolores. "I'm so excited for you. Did you like dancing in Spain?"

"I studied ballet all of my life, but Flamenco... such fire, such passion, it makes me feel alive like no other." Dolores twirled in delight as they passed a barbecue pit where the flames crackled.

CHAPTER TWO

JOY AND SORROW

Sparklers burned brightly in Rico's front yard as Mariachi music filled the air. The clanging of glasses added to the festive atmosphere.

Dolores, blindfolded and still in her wedding dress, wielded a stick in the direction of a white and gold piñata. The delicate fabric of her dress hugged her skin as she twirled around in excitement. She finally hit her target. Party-favors burst from the piñata and children whooped as they scrambled to scoop them up.

Across the yard, Rico was in lively conversation with Mair, Bobby, Jamieson and Morrison and his wife, all with drinks and laughing. Dolores skipped over to her father like a small child and wrapped her arms around him. "It's wonderful. Thank you so much. I wish Mama could have been here."

Rico turned to face her. "I believe in my heart she's looking down on us right now." He gave her a hug. "Where's Teodoro?"

"Over there stuffing his face. He'll need to go on a diet after this is over."

"Go get him. I have a special gift for the two of you. From Mama."

Dolores smiled and ran off. Rico turned back to Mair. "Thanks for all your help. I didn't know how we were ever going to finish setting this up in time."

Mair lightly touched Rico's arm, interrupting his thoughts. Her lips parted to say something, but Dolores returned, accompanied by Teodoro. He was tall and slender with a sophisticated air about him, as if he had seen the world and all its wonders.

"Okay, we're ready," Dolores announced, her voice carrying an air of excitement.

Rico stepped forward to present a small wrapped gift. With eager anticipation, Dolores tore into it, revealing a small round crystal music box adorned with delicate carvings. Inside stood two dancers — one male and one female — poised atop a sparkling surface. As Rico turned the key, the box came to life with a gentle melody, causing the dancers to gracefully spin and twirl in perfect harmony.

"It's exquisite!" said Teodoro, genuinely affected.

"She knew, huh?" said Rico to his daughter.

"Si, Papa. She knew."

Screeching tires. A car filled with gangbangers swerved around the corner. The unsuspecting party-goers were jolted out of their revelry and turned to see the source of the disturbance, their expressions quickly turning from annoyance to fear. As the car careened closer to Rico's house, a series of deafening pops echoed through the air, causing people to duck and scream in terror. Panic set in as another string of lit firecrackers rained down on the yard like fiery missiles. Desperate to catch any identifying details, Bobby and Jamieson strained to catch a glimpse of the license plate before the car disappeared around another corner. The once lively atmosphere was now thick with tension and unease.

"God, Javier, when did it get this bad?!" asked Morrison. "Maybe you should find a better neighborhood."

"No, I need to make this one better." Rico then turned back to the party-goers, "Come on, we're having a party. Everyone's okay. Just stupid kids. Music!" The music picked up again as did the party.

As the day stretched into evening, the guests were exhausted. In the living room, adults lounged and chatted while sipping drinks and listening to soft background music. Rico, Bobby, Jamieson, and Morrison huddled together in a corner, engaged in conversation. Meanwhile, Teodoro sat on a nearby chair next to Mair and Morrison's wife, who were comfortably seated on the loveseat.

Dolores entered wearing a short white sleeveless summer dress with a ruffled full skirt and white, short-heeled pumps. A white rose sat in the cleft of her breasts. The men perked up and sounded their approval, while the women laughed and pretended to be jealous.

Dolores headed straight to Teodoro and Rico hoisted a glass. "To the bride and groom. Good fortune, always."

Dolores slid onto Teodoro's lap and took a sip from his wine glass as the music changed to a wild Spanish beat: Flamenco guitar. Pounding drum. A guest flipped back the rug, exposing the wood floor beneath. The women clapped rhythmically. All eyes were on Dolores. She feigned fatigue. Teodoro urged her onto the floor and Dolores' heels tapped the wood.

She took a moment then flounced her skirt in true Flamenco style. Guests trilled and cheered her on. She beckoned Teodoro onto the floor then danced around him, brushing her body against his. His heels clacked. Fingers snapped. The duet was sensuous as he wrapped her in his arms. Bent her back. Stole a kiss to cheers. Spun her away from him.

The music then became more frenzied. Dolores pulled the rose from her breast and sensually stroked it against her body.

Loud clacks. Fingers snapped. Heels tapped. Another clack —

SMASH! A window shattered. Heads turned.

Dolores still danced.

POP, POP, POP! Bullets pitted the wall. A vase exploded.

As if in slow motion, a petal fell from Dolores' rose. It floated to the floor while guests dived for safety. Rico lunged for Dolores as — POP! Her head whipped back.

The music ended. Dolores's limp body melted into her father's arms. A trickle of blood appeared from under her hairline. Eerie silence — then in that silent aftermath, the tinkle of music. Faint. Distorted. The fallen music box lay on its side but the dancers still twirled.

The weak tune seemingly bled into the beep, beep, beep of a heart monitor. Dolores lay in a hospital bed with her head bandaged, and a respirator breathing for her. A large bouquet of white roses was positioned next to the bed where her father was slumped in a chair, asleep next to her, still holding her hand.

Activities in the hospital surrounded Mair as she sat exhausted in the waiting room. Days later, she would see an anguished Rico through the glass of an office door as he sat listening to a doctor and a patient advocate.

Police officers stood guard at the open front door, their expressions grim as they surveyed the damage inside Rico's once pristine house — now riddled with bullet holes, inside and out, and surrounded by yellow police tape, a stark contrast against the neatly trimmed lawn and flowerbeds. Rico emerged from the house, his arm intertwined with Mair's for support. He carried a small overnight bag as they made their way to her car, parked on the gravel driveway. She was taking him to her secluded home, nestled in a remote rural property.

The ranch-style house sat at the edge of a sprawling meadow, while a large converted barn loomed in the distance. This was where Mair ran her successful business, ShowGun, and where she felt most at peace in the chaos that had unfolded at Rico's house. As they drove away, Rico couldn't help but feel grateful for Mair's friendship and refuge in this trying time.

As the sun set, casting a warm glow through the windows of the ShowGun warehouse, George, the company's manager, could be found hard at work in his wheelchair. He was a man in his 30s with a determined expression and calloused hands from years of handling guns and ammunition. The warehouse itself was an impressive sight, converted from a large barn and filled to the brim with supplies and equipment. Against one wall stood three massive gun safes, their metal doors gleaming in the dim light. On another wall hung a ShowGun banner, proudly displaying their logo alongside a variety of rubber guns and knives. Shelves lined the remaining walls, neatly organized with gun magazines, ammo, and miscellaneous gear. Scattered throughout were autographed movie posters from productions that ShowGun had worked on.

At the center of it all sat an impeccably organized desk with a formidable computer network setup. A photo rested on the corner of the desk, depicting Mair in full military uniform holding a powerful fifty-caliber sniper rifle. Standing beside her were Rico, Morrison, Jamieson, and George himself — still able-bodied in the photo. It served as a reminder of their past successes and the camaraderie they shared as coworkers and friends.

Mair was on the phone. "I left my number with the hospital."

Morrison was at the other end of the line. "How's Javier doing?"

"Resting... finally."

"Anything from Jamieson?"

"He said he or Bobby would call if they have anything. I'm gonna go up to the house to make some tea for Javier. Thanks for checking in."

She hung up. "Let's call it a day," she said to George.

"You got it, boss."

The next day, Jamieson drove to the ShowGun warehouse where he saw workmen load guns and equipment into a large truck. George was taking inventory. Mair exited the warehouse and handed off more equipment to the workmen. "After the drop off at Universal, make that pick up at Warner's. Then back here. I'll have one more load for you."

Jamieson pulled up and exited his car just as the workmen closed up the back of the truck. "Hey George, how ya doing?"

"Great, Jamie." George wheeled himself into the warehouse as Mair and Jamieson went in. He then went off to his station and began assembling a rifle.

"Sorry I'm late," said Jamieson, "was tied up in another one of those morale-boosting meetings... you know, where they tell you what a rotten job we're all doing." He then spotted a space laser gun on a work table. He tested its weight and took aim. "I love this gun. What movie again?"

"Alien Nemesis," George reminded him.

"Right. I loved the part when they shoved the gun down the alien's throat and it started glowing."

Just then, Rico entered looking refreshed. Jamieson put the gun down and turned solemn. "Any word from the hospital?" he asked.

"No," said Rico. "You hear anything?"

"Nothing. No talk on the street. But I did hear there's another gun buy-back in the works."

"They're always bringing that up," Rico said.

"This time it's not just talk."

"Yeah, let's all get in line for a gift certificate or some other shit." Mair said facetiously.

"What gall," said Jamieson, "especially since it was the Feds who lost that gun shipment headed to border patrol." He then noticed that Rico was preoccupied with his own thoughts. "Sorry."

George wheeled across the room behind them with an M16 in his lap.

"If it were up to me, I'd blow them all to—" said Jamieson.

He was interrupted by George shouting, "Test fire!" Everyone covered their ears. George then loaded and pointed the rifle barrel into a test drum. "Fire in the hole." Several big booms were heard as he fired.

Just then, Rico's phone rang. He eagerly answered it but within seconds, his face dropped.

Soon Rico sat at the bedside in the hospital, Teodoro by his side with his leg bandaged, as silent tears spilled down their cheeks. Dolores lay still on the crisp white sheets, her face pallid and peaceful. Mair stood off to the side, her own tears streaming down her face as she struggled to hold herself together. She didn't want to intrude on this delicate moment with her presence, but she couldn't help but show her love and support for the family. Rico reached out a trembling hand towards her, beckoning for her to join them. With heavy steps, she made her way over, her heart breaking for the pain they were all feeling.

Rico then gently picked up the music box and wound it, its delicate tune echoing through the sterile room. The soft melody was soon joined by the rhythmic whooshing of the respirator that kept Dolores alive. The sound was almost comforting in a way, a steady reminder of life amidst the doom.

But then the doctor entered, and all thoughts of comfort vanished. Another tortuous moment passed before Rico motioned for him to proceed with removing Dolores from life support. The room filled with sobs as the machines were turned off and Dolores' heartbeat slowly faded away.

Tears flowed freely as they said their final goodbyes to Dolores, knowing that she was now at peace. It was a flood of emotions — grief, relief, and even a hint of guilt for letting her go. But through it all, there was love — love for Dolores and each other — holding them together in this heart-wrenching moment.

On the day of the funeral, the air was heavy with the scent of freshly cut flowers. The gravesite was adorned with an abundant display of colorful blooms, a beautiful tribute to Dolores' memory. Gathered there were Rico, his arm around Teodoro for support, Mair quietly weeping, Bobby and Jamieson looking somber, and Morrison with his wife by his side. Alongside them stood Rico's relatives and friends, all paying their respects to their beloved Dolores. Councilwoman Park was also among them, a sign of how deeply loved and respected Dolores and her father were in the community.

As the priest gave his eulogy, the crowd fell silent. His words were filled with emotion and reverence for Dolores' life. "Lord God, You gave us Dolores to grow in age and grace. Now You have called her back. We mourn over her loss and struggle to understand Your purpose. May she rest in peace and stand with all the angels and saints." He paused for a moment before continuing, "Eternal rest grant unto Dolores, O Lord, and let perpetual light shine upon her. Amen."

As the ceremony came to an end, it was time for those closest to Dolores to say their final goodbyes. Rico stepped up to the casket first, tears streaming down his face as he placed a single white rose on top. Teodoro followed suit, leaning heavily on his crutches but determined to pay his respects. Mair walked back from the casket and stood next to Rico, offering him comfort as they watched others take their turns. The somber atmosphere hung heavy in the air as each person said their farewells to Dolores or left a small token of love and remembrance.

Outside the grand City Hall building, Mayor Mark Grayson stood tall and imposing at a podium, his chiseled features betraying the weight of responsibility he carried. His silver hair caught the sunlight and framed his sharp jawline as he addressed the gathered reporters and TV crews. Standing next to him was Police Chief Angela Carlotta, her demeanor exuding professionalism and strength despite the tragic events that had brought them here.

As Grayson spoke into a bank of microphones, the crowd of journalists jostled for position, their cameras and microphones thrust forward in anticipation. "Our hearts go out to councilman Javier Rico and his family," Grayson began, his voice firm and resolute. "In times like this, we are often told it's too soon to talk about solutions. But as leaders of this city, it is our duty to act swiftly and decisively to ensure the safety of our communities." He paused briefly before continuing, "That is why we are launching a gun buy-back program and..." His words were drowned out by a barrage of questions from the reporters, eager for more information.

"Do you really believe the gun buy-back will make a difference?" one shouted.

"Have there been any developments in finding the killers of..." another chimed in.

The chaos continued with no concrete answers being given, only promises of action in the future.

When the press conference was concluded, Mayor Grayson and Police Chief Carlotta walked through a corridor inside City Hall. "Well that was brutal," she said. "I can't stand having to play dodgeball with reporters."

"I'd like to tell them what's really going on," said Grayson. "There's no money and the gangs know it."

When they reached Grayson's office, Carlotta said, "By the way, I have as many detectives as I can spare working the case."

"I know. But the problem is what do we do the next time it happens?"

As the sun set and cast a warm glow over Mair's house, Rico and Mair sat at the kitchen table, their cups of tea cradled in their hands. The room was filled with a cozy silence, broken only by the occasional clink of their spoons against their cups. "Teodoro's gone back to Spain," Rico finally spoke up, his voice heavy with emotion. "To be with his family."

Mair got up from her seat and made her way back to the stove to refill their cups. The scent of chamomile and honey filled the air as she poured. As she returned to her seat, she offered a comforting smile to Rico.

"I think it's time for me to go home too," he continued, his gaze lingering on Mair. "But before I leave, I really want to thank you for everything you've done for me."

Mair's face softened with concern as she looked at him. "There's no need for thanks, Javier. You know you're always welcome here." She paused, then added, "You shouldn't be alone tonight. At least stay until morning."

But Rico shook his head with a small smile and stood up from the table. He gently patted Mair's shoulder as he walked past her towards the door. "Thank you again," he said softly before making his way out of the room. As he left, Mair couldn't help but worry about her friend, alone in the quiet night.

The next day, as Rico stepped out of his house, he couldn't help but feel a wave of guilt wash over him. Two men were loading boxes and bags labeled "Veterans of America" onto their truck from his porch. He had promised to donate them months ago, yet here they were, still sitting on his porch. But he couldn't dwell on that now, he had work to do.

At City Hall, Rico found himself once again frustrated on the phone with a detective. It seemed like there was never any progress in finding the culprits behind the shooting at his house that resulted in Dolores' death. "Yes, I'm still here," he sighed into the phone.

The detective's voice came through apologetically. "I'm sorry, Councilman. There just isn't anything new."

Rico could feel his temper rising. "You said you would keep me updated either way."

"I sent a letter just last week, didn't you get it?"

Rico glanced at his inbox and saw the unopened letter in question. "Yes, I see it now. Must have misplaced it. Sorry." The detective assured him that he would be informed of any developments and hung up. Rico placed the unopened letter back in his inbox.

But as he sat surrounded by stacks of reports, his eyes kept drifting towards one in particular — *Gifts for Guns Exchange Program*. Through his office window, he watched people going about their normal lives while he was stuck dealing with the constant crime and violence in his district.

He grabbed the report and stormed into the office of the Chief of Police, surprising Angela Carlotta who was used to greeting scheduled visitors, not unexpected guests. Rico slammed the report down onto her desk. "You know this is all meaningless, right? These guns are the least likely to be used in crimes."

Between clenched teeth, Angela responded, "Between you and me, you're right. But I'm facing over four-hundred gangs with thousands of members."

Rico wanted to scream in frustration. He knew she was right, but he couldn't just sit back and do nothing while his community suffered.

He turned to leave, but Angela called after him. "Javier, we're doing everything we can to find them. I hope you know that. But as far as the gang problem goes, we're all held hostage by budget constraints and legal procedures."

Rico paused, feeling conflicted. He understood the limitations they were up against, but he couldn't help but feel like they needed to think outside the box for once. He pointed at the report on her desk. "People deserve more than empty promises and bureaucratic red tape." There was nothing more to say — both he and Angela knew it. The weight of their responsibilities weighed heavily on both of them, leaving them feeling torn between doing what's best for the community and being constrained by the system.

CHAPTER THREE
THE GATHERING

Rico drove with the report still sitting in his gut — Carlotta's words, the buy-back, all of it. He'd said his piece and it hadn't moved anything. It never did. He turned downtown and that's when he saw it.

A large sign "Gifts for Guns Exchange" flapped against the backdrop of the bustling L.A. Sports Arena in downtown Los Angeles. The arena's towering structure was adorned with flashing lights and advertising banners. But most striking was the sight of guns, large and small, being exchanged for gift certificates — a symbol of hope or delusion.

Dozens of cars filled the parking lot, their metal frames glinting under the harsh sun contrasted by the ones purposely painted matte black or gray. Police vehicles filled the lot, their presence creating a sense of security while dozens of officers stood ready for action, their eyes peeled on drivers, looking for anything suspicious. Ironic considering that under different circumstances they might have regarded those same drivers to be a potential threat.

The police handled the exchange efficiently. They took down reams of information from the gun owners, a constant rustle of papers being filled out and exchanged, and the clink of metal as guns were handed over to the officers and dropped in secured bins set up just for that purpose. The promised gift certificates for gas, restaurant meals or groceries followed. Gun owners' choice. And, not a gangbanger in sight.

Rico drove past the arena and caught sight of a makeshift Army jeep turning into the lot with what looked like a gatling gun mounted on it. He slowed without meaning to, staring at it a beat too long — then let out a short, humorless laugh and shook his head before driving on. He was en route to the city's historic Olvera Street on a special errand.

Olvera Street, as usual, was filled with people seeking deals on goods, from traditional Mexican food to clothing and accessories. Rico was casually dressed and wearing a baseball cap, not wanting to draw attention, as he wended his way through the shoppers.

He entered Lorenzo's Trading Post, a store that sold hats, purses, and other leather goods where Grandma Lorenzo greeted him sadly from behind the counter. "Oh, Javier. I'm so sorry," she said in Spanish.

Rico responded in kind as he took her hand. "Thank you so much for the card. It touched my heart." He paused a moment then said, "I was wondering... is Marco here?" She pointed to the back of the store.

He made his way through the store. In the back, Marco, her 20-year-old grandson, had his head down and was sweeping, the partially removed gang tattoos on his forearms catching the light before he even looked up.

"Marco, hi."

"Oh, hey man," said Marco, as he stopped what he was doing. "I'm sorry about Dolores."

"Thank you," said Rico simply.

"What's going on?" Marco asked.

"I was wondering if you heard anything."

Mr. Lorenzo, Marco's father, entered from the stock room. "Javier! Marco, why didn't you tell me Councilman Rico was here?"

"He just got here, Dad."

Mr. Lorenzo and Rico shook hands. "I was so sorry to hear about Dolores. Please, come, have a seat." He then shouted out to Grandma in Spanish, "We'll be in the back for awhile." Grandma acknowledged with a wave and the men went into the small break room where Mr. Lorenzo poured

Rico a coffee. They sat at a small table, sipping, as Marco stood at the doorway.

"I was hoping Marco might have heard something," said Rico.

"You know, I'm always hoping he hasn't." Mr. Lorenzo set his cup down and looked at it for a moment. "I want my son safe. I also want this neighborhood safe. I just never figured out how to have both at the same time." He exhaled slowly, then looked over to Marco.

Rico looked over too. The young man's hands gripped the broom. He looked down at his tats then to his father and back to Rico. "What do ya need?"

That evening, Rico, Bobby and Jamieson gathered around the dining room table at Mair's house. Coffee cups and glasses sat waiting. The table had just been cleared of dishes, although a few crumbs remained on the table top. Mair entered the room, placing a steaming carafe of coffee and a bottle of whiskey on the table while Bobby quickly swept up the crumbs with his hand and dropped them on his saucer.

"Great meal, Mair," complimented Rico.

"Gave me a chance to practice feeding a horde for Thanksgiving," she replied with a chuckle.

As Rico poured himself some whiskey, he fell into deep thought, staring intently at his glass. Mair noticed the distant look in his eyes and spoke up, "Javier?"

"We need to disrupt their income," Rico announced suddenly, snapping out of his thoughts. "That's a tactic we haven't used enough on gangs."

"Well, we've tried that before and they always bounce back," countered Jamieson. "They're like cockroaches on steroids."

"More like chickenshits," growled Bobby through gritted teeth.

"Some are redeemable though. Look at you," reminded Rico gently.

"I was eight years old!" said Bobby, still holding onto anger from his past experiences with gangs.

In an attempt to lighten the mood, Jamieson poured more whiskey into Bobby's glass. "Here, put some hair on your chest."

Rico let out a heavy sigh before continuing, "I just heard that the gangs are going after the buy-back guns."

"How ironic. Legal guns ending up in the hands of criminals. Our government at its best," spat Bobby bitterly.

Rico winced slightly at the sting of those words but quickly pushed it aside as he took a sip of his drink. "And on top of it all, they already have buyers lined up."

"You know this, how?" asked Jamieson.

"How are they planning to get their hands on the guns?" added Mair.

"They're going to intercept them on the way to the smelting facility," explained Rico, his face grim.

"That's pretty ballsy but also pretty stupid," remarked Mair. "Won't security be tight?"

"Actually, with all the furloughs, there won't be as many cops on duty," replied Jamieson.

Rico turned to Mair and said, "Which is why I was hoping you could help us."

"Me? What can I do?" questioned Mair, surprised by the request.

"The council has the ability to hire companies as independent contractors, just like the feds did with Blackwater. It helps with liability too," Rico explained.

"I bet." agreed Mair wryly.

"I have an idea for setting up a sting operation," continued Rico.

The room fell into silence as they all considered the potential risks and rewards of such a plan. "I'm listening," said Mair finally.

"As a legit company with the right equipment and connections..." began Rico.

"I see where you're going with this. We can keep costs down by using my resources," finished Mair, catching onto Rico's plan.

"And we all have good military contacts," added Rico, gesturing around the table. "Plus, I can get you instated immediately."

"Instated." She let that sit a moment. "You mean like deputies? Because that's the part where I start wondering if you've lost your mind."

"Yes. You've already been vetted by the military and only two council signatures are needed. I have the second one on standby," explained Rico confidently.

"I don't think Bobby and I can get involved," spoke up Jamieson.

"You two can serve as city advisors, as required by protocol. Everything will be strictly by the book," assured Rico.

Jamieson and Bobby exchanged a wary glance before Mair suddenly burst out, "Am I the only one who thinks this could be crazy dangerous? What if we go after them and then they come after us?"

"It's a valid concern," acknowledged Rico. "Maybe this is too much to ask."

All eyes turned to Mair as she contemplatively sipped on her coffee, now spiked with whiskey. After a moment of silence, Rico spoke up once more, "You know Morrison and you know the kind of connections he has. Not to mention Jamieson's own contacts. This would be a chance to hit 'em where it hurts." Mair was almost convinced. She poured herself another shot of whiskey and took a long sip, deep in thought.

In Councilwoman Park's office the following day, Park and Rico gathered around her computer screen. "They'll be officially added to the system by the end of today," she announced. "Who do you want to list as their advisers?"

"Sergeant Mark Jamieson is our liaison officer."

Park typed in the name and clicked the print button. "Great. I just need your signature." Rico grinned and signed the form, grateful for Park's continued support.

Under the dim glow of a single streetlight, in the heart of a rundown neighborhood where all the shops had long since closed for the night, a solitary figure made her way to her car. The woman's appearance was altered with a different hairstyle and a hat, but there was no mistaking her as Mair. As she walked, the sound of footsteps echoed behind her. She turned, catching a glimpse of a shadow darting into a nearby doorway. Her heart raced as she quickened her pace.

The footsteps continued, now matching her own in rhythm and growing louder. Mair broke into a run, scanning her surroundings for any sign of danger. In the corner of her eye, she spotted another figure heading straight towards her from the left. Without hesitation, she reached for her handbag and retrieved her gun while still on the move. As she reached her car, she dove onto the hood and slid over to the other side, hitting the pavement hard. With quick reflexes, she aimed her gun and fired multiple shots from behind the safety of the vehicle.

The figure on her left returned fire, shattering the car window and sending shards of glass flying towards Mair. She ducked instinctively before returning fire once more. The gunman fell to the ground with a thud. But more shots were coming her way. Using the car as cover, she crawled towards the back and swiftly reloaded her gun before taking out the other two men who were approaching, firing rounds at her.

Amidst the chaos and noise of gunfire, shattered glass and torn metal, a voice suddenly yelled "Cut!" The scene was actually taking place on a film studio backlot where numerous crew members bustled about their various tasks amidst cameras, sound equipment and tangled cables.

As the director called for a break, the two downed gunmen got back up, dusting off their clothes while the actress, who bore a striking resemblance to Mair, went over to embrace her. The two women shared a laugh as they relaxed and chatted during the filming of their latest action-packed scene.

Rico, Jamieson, and Bobby, stood to the side and watched as the rest of the crew wrapped up their work. Mair gathered the guns and carefully placed them in cases. Rico broke away from the commotion and made his way over to her.

"It looked like you took a hard fall. Are you okay?" he asked with concern.

Mair replied with a teasing grin, "Would you be asking me that if I were a man?"

"Of course I would," said Rico with a chuckle.

As they conversed, the assistant director called out to Mair, reminding her of their early call time for tomorrow: 4:30 AM. She acknowledged and then led Rico, Bobby, and Jamieson down a backlot street to their weapons' staging area: an old Western town with its iconic saloon. Upon entering through the swinging doors, Mair handed off the gun cases to George, who was intently watching the news on his laptop. The anchorman's voice filled the air, reporting on a recent murder:

"Two men were arrested today for the murder of Maria Guttierez, a Compton grocery store clerk killed earlier this week."

The group turned their attention to the screen as surveillance footage showed a bandit shooting 30-year-old Guttierez after she had given him money. A second man stood guard at the door.

"Jesus Christ!" exclaimed George.

The anchorman continued, "Guttierez leaves behind three children ages two, four, and five. It was learned today that she was a former gang member and that may have been a motive for the murder."

Rico shook his head. A grocery store clerk. Three kids. He thought of the Kims, of Dolores, of every person just trying to get through a day in a neighborhood nobody else wanted to think about. Same story. Different name.

Bobby and Jamieson expressed their disgust. George closed his laptop and handed out sodas from a nearby cooler as they all took a seat.

"ShowGun is officially city-approved," announced Rico.

"From taxpayer to volunteer, to citizen army," added Bobby with a hint of pride. But his tone quickly changed as he switched into TV commercial mode, "Gangs got you down? Are you fed up with drive-bys, corner drug deals, and endless crime? For peace of mind, call ShowGun."

"Hey, cut that shit," said Jamieson sternly. "It's not funny."

Bobby looked over at Rico, "Sorry."

There was an uncomfortable silence briefly until Mair spoke up again. "One of my customers told me about an old lady in his building... She's gotta be around ninety... She said, and I quote, 'I wish I could take a baseball bat to those bastards.'"

"I wish *I* could do something to help," offered George.

"Don't worry. We'll figure something out for you," assured Mair.

"Definitely," agreed Rico.

Jamieson paused from drinking his soda, "Some guys at work have been talking about a gang hangout near the border. The bangers call it the Alamo."

"That's worth checking out," said Rico thoughtfully. "But right now, we have the gun buy-back problem. I'm still waiting on Morrison."

Jamieson pulled out a small notepad, "You wouldn't believe how many bored retirees want to be a part of this."

"How about Schizwicki?" suggested George.

Bobby gave him a questioning look.

"We want to stop them," clarified Rico, "not blow them up!"

Jamieson, Bobby and George all exchanged a look — blowing them up actually sounded good to them.

CHAPTER FOUR
CALL IN THE MARINES

Downstate at Camp Pendleton Marine Base, it was mid-morning. On a rifle range, four targets, eight hundred yards downrange were being viewed through a spotting scope. Suddenly, there was a muffled gunshot and a bullet struck low on a target.

A voice sounded, "Carmello, you're a skosh low, and you haven't allowed for the two minute wind out there. Check the mirage... the vegetation." Morrison sat on a bench, looking through the spotting scope that was set on a tripod. There was another muffled shot. "Richards, I saw a little dust on that shot. Your wet-down is drying out. Fix it."

A muffled shot followed. "Balboa, you ain't reading the wind so hot, either." Morrison cocked an ear. Another muffled shot. "Ortega, you're working the bolt too hard. The noise could wake the dead... then you can join them." There was an exasperated sigh as Morrison stood. "Okay that's it for now. Break for lunch. Meet back here at thirteen-thirty."

Ten yards in front of him, parts of the vegetation rose and four snipers in their twenties, wearing ghillie suits with burlap and foliage attached, stood with their sniper rifles dressed with suppressors and scopes, also camouflaged.

One sniper addressed the man to his right, "Maybe you outta put a suppressor on that bolt of yours. Almost broke my eardrum."

"Yeah, and next time get yours up higher. You know how to get it up, don't ya?"

The third sniper laughingly said, "Higher and harder," as he started singing, "That's the way... ahuh, ahuh she likes it..." The other Snipers joined in singing as they moved off, "... ahuh, ahuh... That's the way... ahuh, ahuh ..."

Morrison checked his watch then quickly headed in another direction.

Rico was already waiting when Morrison reached his base office.

He sat at his desk with Rico sitting opposite. "I'll make some calls," said Morrison. "I do know one guy off the top of my head. You remember that martial arts guy who got kicked out of boot camp?"

"What about him?"

"He's in L.A. now. Owns a dojo. I hear he lets bangers in to take lessons just so he can kick their asses hard enough to put them in the hospital."

"Sounds motivated."

That night, Rico used the intel from Morrison to pay the dojo guy a visit. He took Bobby with him as he drove downtown, past a row of storefronts, many covered in vibrant graffiti. "There it is," said Bobby.

They parked in front of the only storefront *without* graffiti, "Tanaka's Dojo," and peered through the clean glass window. A dozen blackbelts, ages 20s-30s, led by Michael Tanaka who was about Morrison's age, engaged in a finely-tuned drill of self-defense techniques against a knife. Half of the students held knives while the others wielded Kali sticks. The movements were fluid and swift as they switched back and forth, each taking turns being on the offensive.

When the drill ended, Rico and Bobby entered the dojo. The students lined up in front of Tanaka and bowed respectfully before standing at attention. Then, one by one, the students with knives put their weapons away by throwing them at a large thick wooden board with a painted figure target. Each knife landed perfectly in the center mass.

"Interesting," remarked Rico as he observed the students' skilled handling of real knives.

Bobby shook his head. "Those guys are crazy."

As Rico and Bobby made their way across the spacious dojo, the students worked diligently to clean up. The room was filled with the sound of bodies shifting and equipment being put away, all while the faint scent of sweat and incense lingered in the air. "Hey, Michael Tanaka," Rico called out when they reached the instructor. Tanaka turned to face them, his gaze cold and calculating. "Can we talk privately?"

After a brief moment of consideration, Tanaka led them into his office. Bobby closed the door behind them as Tanaka removed his damp Gi jacket, revealing a stunning display of colorful Japanese Koi tattoos on his chest and back. He wiped away the sweat with a towel before slipping on a simple white t-shirt. "What do you want?" he asked, his tone guarded.

"We're here to offer you an opportunity," Rico stated boldly. "We've heard that you don't take kindly to gang members."

Tanaka's expression remained unreadable. "And where did you hear that?" he asked.

"From a Marine who remembers you from boot camp," answered Rico.

"And did he happen to mention that I was kicked out?" Tanaka raised an eyebrow.

"He might have mentioned it," conceded Rico.

"And did he tell you why?" Tanaka pressed further.

Rico hesitated before responding, "Excessive brutality. Lethal use of nunchucks. Something like that."

"Something like that..." Tanaka repeated, his eyes narrowing. "Which gives you some idea of what I might do to guys coming into my dojo asking for my help in starting fires."

Bobby bristled at Tanaka's words. "I thought you might want to help someone who tried to help you."

Tanaka's gaze shifted to Bobby. "What are you talking about?" he asked with genuine curiosity.

Bobby pointed to Rico. "He went to bat for you and got into some deep shit over it."

Tanaka's expression softened slightly. "Yeah? I didn't know that."

"Well, now you do," said Bobby.

Rico kept his eyes on Tanaka. "Doesn't matter. Ancient history."

"So what makes you think I'd be interested in whatever bullshit the government is dreaming up these days?" Tanaka challenged.

"The city and the military are two different animals," said Rico.

"The city doesn't do shit in this neighborhood," Tanaka scoffed. "Let the cops earn their pay. I've got my own problems to deal with."

"Christ, what an attitude!" Bobby couldn't help but exclaim. Rico shot him a warning look to cool it.

Tanaka turned back to Bobby, "Hey, I couldn't pick you out of a crowd of one, and now you're pissed because I haven't jumped at your 'opportunity'?"

"I understand," said Rico. "It's just that Morrison thought you'd be valuable to our team."

"Morrison?" Tanaka was impressed.

Inside the ShowGun warehouse, Mair was off to the side, alternately breaking down a script and keeping eyes on the activity as Jamieson, Bobby, four of Jamieson's seasoned SWAT men all aged in their 30s-50s, stood at a large work table in deep discussion.

"I hear Morrison's got us some additional men," reported Bobby with excitement.

"Yeah, one of them's Wilson," confirmed Jamieson.

"Wilson? The guy with the two point one mile kill shot?"

Jamieson nodded solemnly, and the others present were visibly awestruck.

Just then, Rico entered the warehouse with five formidable Marines, all aged in their 40s-50s. They were physically imposing and exuded an aura of strength and experience. Rico made introductions, pointing out each man by name. "Hey everybody, this is Rossen, Hughes, McAllister, Lewis, and Wilson."

The group exchanged firm handshakes and greetings, but Bobby was immediately drawn to Wilson. "You're Wilson, right?" he asked eagerly.

"Yep."

Bobby shook his hand vigorously. "Wow. Thank you!" He then moved off to join the others, leaving Wilson slightly bewildered.

Rico motioned for everyone to gather around as he and Jamieson began laying out the plan for their upcoming operation. "For you new guys," Rico explained, "ShowGun's operations are sanctioned by the city. But for this particular mission, Jamieson will be taking the lead."

Jamieson stepped up to the monitors and tapped the aerial view of the intersection. "Our Intel is that the gangs are going to hit the buy-back shipment at Euclid and Eighth. Ground zero." He pointed out the freeway exit, the stop sign, the approach routes. "Decoy truck comes in from the north. They'll pick it up here, follow it to here. That's where we take them."

One of the new Marines, Rossen, studied the layout and leaned in. "How many hostiles and what's our window once they move on the truck?"

Jamieson looked at him evenly. "Seven, maybe eight. Window's tight — thirty seconds from the time they box us in." Rossen nodded once and stepped back.

Across the room, Wilson had said nothing. He stood apart from the group, arms folded, eyes moving quietly over the monitors with the unhurried patience of a man who had done this in places far worse than Los Angeles.

Meanwhile, at his station off to the side, George already had the layout mapped on his screen, the route marked, positions color-coded. He looked up and caught Rico's eye, gave a small nod. Got it.

As they all huddled together over maps and aerial views on TV monitors, Jamieson and Rico laid out every remaining detail of their plan before handing it over to the team to execute.

It started at the LAPD motor pool warehouse complex, when a mammoth door rolled up and a large LAPD truck was ready to roll out. Jamieson and Bobby, dressed as uniformed officers, hopped in the front. Two of Jamieson's men jumped in back and closed it up. The LAPD decoy truck then left the facility and rolled onto a street. The plan was to follow the usual route to the meltdown facility.

It passed some parked cars as it neared the freeway entrance. There, five gangbangers in a white van eyed the truck while one spoke on a cell phone. As anticipated, the van pulled out and followed the decoy truck. A few cars back was an unmarked car with another two of Jamieson's men. It followed the gangbangers' van.

Standing by at ground zero were two teams made up of Morrison's men. On the "go" signal, team one would come in from the north while the other would come in from the south.

The decoy truck, van and unmarked cars all drove down the freeway.

Overlooking ground zero, on high ground, was Wilson surveilling the intersection through the scope of his fifty-caliber sniper rifle.

The decoy truck exited the freeway and turned onto a road with little traffic and fewer structures. It pulled up to a stop sign. Suddenly, a car with two gangbangers pulled up and blocked the front of the decoy truck while the white banger van slammed to a stop behind the truck. Bangers piled out and ran to the back of the truck with bolt cutters.

The two bangers from the car took position on either side of the truck and motioned for Jamieson and Bobby to exit. Both, wearing ear pieces, were forced to the front of the truck while the bangers stood on the curb, next to a fire hydrant.

"Now," whispered Wilson into their ear pieces.

Jamieson and Bobby hit the dirt as Wilson's bullet hit the fireplug that exploded. The sound of metal on metal reverberated through the air. It blew the bangers off their feet, dousing them with water. When the other bangers swung open the back doors of the decoy truck, Jamieson's men burst out.

Two of the bangers raised their guns to fire. Not quick enough. Jamieson's men blasted both of them with their M4 carbines. The other bangers quickly dropped their weapons.

With his sniper scope, Wilson watched as Jamieson trained his gun on the injured and dazed bangers while Bobby skillfully zip-tied them. All the backup cars then rolled onto the scene. Mission accomplished.

A few days later, at the bustling downtown Los Angeles courthouse, a convoy of police vans and cars pulled up to a side entrance. The buy-back bangers, handcuffed and escorted by officers, were perp-walked past a frenzy of news crews and reporters all scrambling for the best view.

Inside her spacious office, Police Chief Carlotta frantically juggled phone calls while her assistants fielded constant interruptions from ringing phones and fax machines spitting out papers. Her voice rose in frustration as she barked orders into the receiver, "I don't care if they *are* juveniles! Leak their names to the press!"

She slammed down the phone and gestured for the two detectives standing outside her door. "Do we have their parents here?"

"Downstairs... with lawyers," replied one of them.

"That was quick."

The second detective scoffed, *"He was such a good boy."*

Carlotta's face twisted in anger. "Fuck that." She began stacking papers into a folder, preparing herself for what was sure to be a fierce fight in the courtroom as well as in the public square.

Inside Gangbanger Central, better known as Naldo's warehouse, Naldo sat hunched at a desk in his grungy office that was on a loft overlooking the warehouse floor below. He was on the phone and watching a TV news report that showed his men being hustled into the courthouse. "I'm sorry, Mr. Salazar," he said into the phone. "It was just one of those weird fucking accident things."

Salazar's voice boomed out at him. "I think the concept you're trying to impart is that it was a *coincidence*. Is that what you're trying to tell me?"

"Yeah, yes, that's what I mean."

Salazar was a slick, 45-year old cartel drug distributor, ruthless and unrelenting. He paced the up-scale office-den of his well-appointed mansion somewhere south of the border. In the background, the same TV news images were playing. "Naldo, usually you get things done on time. That's what I like about you and why I continue to do business with you. But I can just as easily forge another relationship with one of your competitors. So let me be clear. You get me my guns or you and your homies are going to be spending the rest of your lives in wheelchairs sipping on straws. The next time I see any of your fucking crew on TV, you're done."

"I understand, Mr. Salazar. I'll get your guns."

"Make it quick. I have cross border commitments."

Naldo slammed the phone down and paced back and forth, his mind racing with conflicting thoughts of anger and guilt. In frustration, he grabbed the phone and hurled it across the room, unsure of what to do next.

City Hall stood tall and imposing, its steps leading up to the entrance crowded with onlookers and supporters eagerly awaiting a press conference. Mayor Grayson, accompanied by Police Chief Carlotta, stepped in front of the cameras as polite applause filled the air.

"Yesterday was a triumph for our city," declared Grayson with a confident smile. "Thanks to our coordinated efforts, seven members of a notorious gang were arrested and over four hundred deadly weapons have been removed from our streets and destroyed."

He gestured for Carlotta to speak, and she stepped forward with her usual air of authority. "This is just the beginning. Our department will continue to use every means at our disposal to combat crime and protect our citizens."

A bold female reporter raised her hand. "Can you confirm the involvement of ShowGun, a private company, in preventing the gun shipment attack?"

Grayson responded smoothly, "As part of our innovative approach to law enforcement, we have utilized independent contractors in some cases. Yesterday's success is a testament to the effectiveness of our strategy."

"I've heard that council members Rico and Park played key roles in initiating this plan," pressed the reporter.

The mayor's press aide quickly intervened with a practiced smile. "We appreciate all contributions to our mission of making our city safer. That concludes this press conference."

CHAPTER FIVE

ONE MORE DOWN

Rico sat in the back of the cab and watched the city roll past. The press aide's sign-off was still ringing in his ears — *we appreciate all contributions* — which was the polished way of saying don't push it. He let it go. Tonight wasn't for pushing. Tonight was for the people who'd actually shown up.

Rico, Mair, Jamieson, Morrison and his wife Cheryl, George, and Bobby with his current girlfriend all sat at a large table in the bustling neighborhood restaurant. The lively chatter of other patrons filled the air and the clinking of silverware against dishes could be heard as busboys cleared their table and refilled drinks. In the background, a video replay of the bangers' perp-walk played on Bobby's phone, capturing everyone's attention. The footage showed one of the bangers with his jacket over his head, struggling against a cop who pulled it away. As the camera zoomed in on his face, it revealed a smirking expression and a glint of gold from his dental grill. He defiantly mouthed words 'Fuck You,' that were promptly bleeped by the network, before tripping on the guy in front of him and falling to the ground. The group erupted into laughter as they watched the banger's grill break off upon impact, causing Bobby to howl with delight. It was a moment of comedic relief amid the tension of their recent encounter with the bangers.

"Darts, anyone?" Jamieson took the last gulp of his drink.

"I'm in," said George.

Morrison's wife slapped her husband's arm. "Let's team up."

The four moved towards the bar and the dartboard just as a female singer joined the band. "For all the lovers out there," she said.

Bobby's girlfriend pulled him over to the dance floor while Rico and Mair were the only ones left at the table. "I'm working on…" started Rico.

Mair was moved by the music. "I have a better idea. How about we dance?"

"She said it was for *lovers*."

Mair responded jokingly, "We can pretend." Rico was both pleasantly surprised and unsure. Nevertheless he went with the flow and followed her to the dance floor where Bobby was ogling the singer.

They found a spot on the floor. Rico settled a hand at her waist. She rested her fingers lightly on his shoulder, and for a moment neither of them said a word, just moved together with the music. He glanced down at her. She was already looking up at him. Neither looked away.

"What are you doing?" his girlfriend spewed at Bobby.

"What do you mean, what am I doing?"

"You can't keep your eyes off her."

"Off who?"

"Listen if you're gonna play dumb, then you're too dumb for me."

Rico and Mair watched as the girlfriend stormed off and Bobby hurried after her.

"Just think, that could be us in a few years," Mair said. Rico burst out laughing.

At the dartboard, George's aim was impeccable. His darts flew through the air with ease, each one landing perfectly in the bullseye. Morrison couldn't believe how lucky George was on this particular day. "Okay, that's enough," he said with a teasing smile. "I'm checking your chair." As Morrison playfully patted down George's wheelchair, the rest of their friends erupted into laughter. "I know you've got this thing rigged," Morrison joked. "No one can be that good."

Amidst their laughter, Jamieson joined in by poking fun at Morrison's constant excuses for losing. "Yeah, you need another excuse to keep losing," he quipped.

But George wasn't fazed by their banter. He simply leaned back in his chair and grinned at them all. "Morrison, you're only upset because I can sit here relaxed while you have to stand," he teased back, causing everyone to go quiet for a moment before bursting into laughter again. It was all in good fun among friends.

Back at the table, Rico and Mair sat huddled, their voices low and animated as they chatted.

The dart players approached cautiously, unsure if they should interrupt the intimate moment. But Rico and Mair noticed them and broke away from each other with welcoming smiles.

"Come on," said Rico.

"Sit down," invited Mair.

The dart players eagerly rejoined them at the table, their laughter blending in with the lively ambiance of the restaurant. They all clinked glasses and raised their voices in celebration, enjoying each other's company and reveling in a job well done.

Back at his day job, Rico found himself in Council-woman Park's tidy office. The space was meticulously organized, with stacks of papers neatly arranged on her desk and small potted plants carefully placed in various corners. Sunlight poured through the windows, casting a warm glow on the furniture and illuminating Rico's features as he sat across from her.

"I have to admit," she said, admiringly. "I think the opposition was greatly *disappointed* by your success."

"They're only interested in glory without putting in any real effort," Rico shrugged.

"How was it working with Ms. Carling?"

"Couldn't have been better. She's incredibly knowledgeable and has a top-notch team supporting her. Her manager's a genius when it comes to crunching numbers."

"Perhaps we should hire him to work on our budget," Councilwoman Park mused. "But seriously, Javier — the council's not big enough for what you can do and you know it. When are you going to stop dragging your feet on the mayor's race?"

"I'm not sure what to say to that," Rico let out a half-smile.

"Don't be modest. You know exactly what to say and people listen when you speak."

"I can't focus on that right now."

"But you should," Park urged.

Rico shifted uncomfortably in his seat. "I'll consider it… oh, speaking of money. Let's make sure ShowGun gets paid," he reminded.

"I've already submitted the necessary paperwork. It's just a matter of accounting reviewing and cutting the check."

"Thanks for staying on top of it," Rico said gratefully as he rose from his seat.

"It's my pleasure," Councilwoman Park smiled warmly as she waved him off. As Rico exited her office, he couldn't shake off the feeling that, as mayor, there was more at stake than just balancing budgets and approving projects for the city council. How would he use his power and influence? And who would ultimately benefit from it all? These were questions he couldn't ignore for much longer.

Naldo perched on the wooden loft outside his office, surveying the bustling work area below. The clang of metal and the whir of machinery filled the air as workers, ranging from young teenagers to seasoned adults in their 30s, tirelessly dismantled cars and trucks. Upon closer inspection, it was clear that this was no ordinary chop shop — hidden amid the scattered car parts were guns secreted away beneath panels and upholstery. The smell of oil and sweat permeated the space, adding to the gritty atmosphere of Gangbanger Central. From his vantage point, Naldo could see everything unfolding below with sharp clarity, like a bird watching its prey from a safe distance. This was his domain, and he ruled over it with a firm determination that matched the cold, hard steel of the weapons being prepared for use on the streets.

Naldo whistled to get Big Frankie's attention then motioned toward his office. As the big guy moved to the stairs, two others followed, Perez and Cruz. When they entered, they found Naldo on edge.

"Everything's on schedule boss," said Big Frankie.

"The whole shipment?"

Perez shuffled his feet, not wanting to answer.

"Salazar gave me two days… but first there's this little coincidence thing we need to talk about. You know… the kind caused by some ratfucker."

"Whatcha talkin' 'bout?" asked Perez totally clueless.

"Rats squealing to cops. Tell your crew to keep their eyes and ears open and their mouth shut."

Naldo pointed to Big Frankie and Cruz. "Now, get back to work." They left without closing the door behind them. Naldo slammed it shut then closed the blinds and turned to Perez. "We need to do something special. There's a big spot in the valley my cousin keeps telling me about. We'll get less guns but they'll be new and we can grab a ton a bullets and clips."

"I know the store. It's got a shitloada security and those concrete things. You'll never get a truck close to it," warned Perez.

"Which is why they won't be expecting us. And there won't be no more fucking coincidences."

The neon lights of the gun store illuminated the night, beckoning Naldo and his crew to make their move. They pulled up in one of their vans, its engine rumbling softly as it slowed near the large brick store. Concrete barriers across the front were meant to deter thieves, but Naldo and his gang were not easily deterred.

Instead of directly approaching the gun store, they drove around the corner to the Valley Thrift Store. The shop was closed, just as they had planned. The van parked and a group of bangers piled out, eager to get to work. Meanwhile, the driver kept watch as a lookout.

With ease, they broke into the thrift store and quickly disabled the old alarm system before it could even sound. Racks of clothing and shelves of home furnishings were pushed aside as they made their way to a back room. Using tools like drills and hammers, Perez and his crew worked to break through the wall that separated them from their target. To muffle the noise, some bangers held a mattress up while others shined flashlights onto their work.

After what seemed like hours, the wood and plaster finally gave way, revealing a solid brick wall on the other side. This was the back of Porter's Gun Shop, which was conveniently buttressed against the thrift store. Undeterred, Naldo and his crew continued to attack the sturdy wall with sledgehammers until they created a large hole. With adrenaline pumping through his veins, Perez ordered one masked man to enter the gun shop through the breach they had created.

The masked guy worked on disabling the alarm system from a panel inside the shop office while a second masked man rushed in with a paintball gun and shot out all the surveillance cameras. Perez, with a cellphone, headed to the front window. He ducked and kept watch, heart thumping wildly. The last thing he wanted was to let the boss down again. The rest of the gang rushed in and loaded firearms into gun cases and duffel bags. Others grabbed the ammo. One guy dropped a gun on the floor.

"Will you fuckin' be careful. He wants em new lookin'," said Perez.

Another banger spotted a case filled with fancy knives. That jerk grabbed a bunch and put them into a duffel bag along with a smaller knife in his pocket.

Perez spoke into his cellphone. "Still clear?"

The lookout's voice came back, smooth and flat. "Crystal." Their word. Had been for years. Meant nothing to worry about. Meant keep moving.

The men moved the packed-up duffel bags and gun cases back through the broken walls then piled their spoils just inside the front door of the Valley Thrift.

Perez asked the lookout, "We good to go?"

"Yeah."

"Okay, back it in."

The bangers opened the doors and the van backed up to the front door. Simultaneously, six squad cars screeched to a halt, lighting up the bangers. Cops poured out of the vehicles, weapons drawn and trained on the group. Rico and Jamieson emerged from one of the cars, their sharp eyes taking in the scene. Bobby emerged from the van with their lookout, who was now handcuffed and under control. He held the lookout's cellphone up to his mouth, his voice low and dangerous as he spoke into it. "Now this time," he growled, "tell him things aren't so crystal."

Back at the warehouse, after hearing about the latest fuck up, Naldo could be heard screaming his lungs out, "Fuuuuuccccckkkkk!" His furious yell could be heard echoing off the walls.

Suddenly, a telephone was hurled out of his office, sailing over the heads of the workers below. The phone crashed into the windshield of a shiny car that Big Frankie was working on, shattering the glass and denting the metal. The sound of metal scraping against metal filled the air as everyone paused and looked around, unsure of what to do next.

Naldo stood in his office, his chest heaving with anger, while Big Frankie let out a string of curses under his breath as he surveyed the damage.

CHAPTER SIX
GAME DAY

Thanksgiving had rolled around and the porch at Mair's house was lavishly decorated for autumn. Vibrant orange pumpkins and golden corn stalks adorned every corner; a string of leaves was draped around the railing, and a colorful wreath hung on the front door.

Bobby, Jamieson, and George were gathered around the dining room table, their laughter and chatter mingling with the faint sound of a football pre-game playing on TV in the living room. That's where Morrison had planted himself.

In the kitchen, Rico helped Mair with the turkey while Morrison's wife Cheryl bustled about, expertly plating the various side dishes for the meal. Bobby watched and poured himself a drink, savoring the camaraderie of this special holiday gathering.

"I still don't understand why you didn't ask your girlfriend to come," Mair said to Bobby.

"She promised her sister she'd visit for the holidays."

"Oh, so why didn't you go with her?"

"Serving spoon?" interrupted Cheryl.

Mair pointed to a drawer.

"To New York to visit her crazy sister and their three kids during the holidays? No way, no thanks. Besides, I think we're breaking up."

Rico chuckled, "He *thinks* they're breaking up!"

Everyone got a good laugh from that. Cheryl moved to the dining table with her plates as George entered the kitchen with Jamieson who was still relishing the banger take-down. "The look on that punk's face. I just can't get that out of my mind."

George got more soda from the fridge and Mair asked incredulously, "Isn't there enough inside?"

"Morrison drank most of it," Jamieson said. "He's practicing for another pissing contest with Schizwicki."

Most of them laughed as Morrison yelled out, "I heard that!"

Rico said, "Now that's funny."

The turkey and remaining fixings were ready for service prompting Mair to say, "Let's go!"

"That looks great," said Rico. Mair wore a shy smile that he failed to detect. He then hoisted the turkey and brought it into the dining room where everyone took their places. Rico's first official action as head of the table was to raise a glass. "To good friends."

"Good friends," said Mair as she raised hers.

Morrison added, "Definitely."

The team started to drink. Rico paused, his glass still raised, and looked around the table for a moment. "And to making a difference."

"Yeah, let's do it again sometime," said Jamieson.

"Let's not have to," said Rico.

"Amen to that!" came the refrain as they all took a gulp or sip of their chosen beverage.

After the hearty meal, the atmosphere in the room was rowdy as the Thanksgiving Day football game on TV ended and the group re-lived the action in copious detail. Empty beer bottles littered the tables.

The local news came on, barely heard over the chaos. The insert on the TV screen showed Naldo talking to the camera, his eyes peering out from behind a fitted skeleton bandanna covering the lower half of his face. The voice of a local anchorman accompanied the footage. "The gang video released just this morning was averaging a thousand hits a minute before it was pulled from YouTube."

The news now grabbed everyone's attention. The video went full screen revealing Naldo waving a handgun. His curse words were bleeped by the network. "...safe in your f***ing homes, watchin' stupid f***ing games, eatin' turkey and 'punk-in' pies '. Know what I served up for f***ing Thanksgiving Day? A f***ing rat. Wanna see my rat?" As he spoke, the TV camera zoomed out to reveal a struggling, tied up guy with a sack on his head. He wore a white tank top and tattoos on his arms. Some had been partially removed. "Let me show you how I cook my rat."

Rico now recognized the tattoos. "Oh, my God," he said softly.

On the TV screen, Naldo moved the handgun to the guy's temple. The screen then went black amid a shot. BAM! The anchorman's smooth voice ended the story and transitioned into a mindless commercial, a jarring interruption to the intense moment just witnessed.

"Just when it was getting good," Bobby said.

Rico's stomach twisted in knots and his heart raced.

"They're always doing shit like that," said Jamieson.

The room fell into a tense silence as everyone's attention turned to Rico's demeanor. "That was Marco," he stated through gritted teeth, his eyes flickering with anger and pain. "The same kid who helped us get the information on the buy-back truck and the gun store." As Rico stormed out of the room, Mair caught Jamieson's gaze, her expression a mix of shock and guilt.

"He never told me anything about his contacts," Jamieson said. "You?" Mair shook her head 'no' as her eyes filled with tears.

At Gangbanger Central, the atmosphere buzzed with tense energy as Naldo's men went about their various tasks. Their movements were quick and jittery, their eyes constantly darting around or locking onto each other in silent communication. Four large, armed men stood guard over them, their steely gazes following every move made by the gang members. The air was thick with tension and fear, each person acutely aware of the volatile atmosphere surrounding them.

In the dimly lit office, Salazar watched with satisfaction as his two goons worked Naldo over. The sound of flesh meeting flesh was punctuated by Naldo's grunts of pain. His face was a bloody mess, but he was still conscious, tied to a chair in the center of the room.

The goons paused for a moment, wiping sweat from their brows as they caught their breath. Salazar pulled up a chair and sat in front of Naldo, holding up his hand to silence him. A glint of metal caught the light as his bodyguard placed a gun in his hand.

"Now, what did I tell you?" Salazar pointed the gun at Naldo's head, the barrel cool against his skin.

"I solved the problem... like you always tell me to," Naldo stammered, fear etched in his voice.

"And since when do you air your dirty laundry in public? Over the Internet, no less?" Salazar's voice was cold and calculated.

"I needed to send a message. You know..." Naldo trailed off, realizing he had made a grave mistake.

"And now we've got another problem because you've let everyone know that my territory is up for grabs because I have imbeciles working for me." Salazar's tone was filled with disgust.

"I'm sorry. I didn't..." Naldo started to apologize.

"Think?" Salazar finished for him, his finger tightening on the trigger of the gun.

Salazar then got up, looked out the window at the activity below and contemplated his next step. He turned back to Naldo and handed the gun back to his bodyguard. Naldo looked relieved for a moment until Salazar let the goons go at it again. Salazar then signaled for them to stop.

"I'm giving you one last chance to get it right." The goons untied Naldo and knocked him out of the chair. Salazar dropped a piece of paper onto the desk. "That's where you're sending your next message. And don't make me come back to this shithole."

On his way out of the office, Salazar brushed past Cruz who appeared at the door, unseen by Naldo who was now on his knees struggling to get up. Naldo's hands clenched and unclenched at his sides as he watched Salazar go, his jaw working like he was chewing on something he couldn't swallow.

Under his breath, Naldo muttered, "I can't wait for you to come back to this shithole."

Cruz backed out of sight, giving Naldo a chance to recover. Then through blackened, swollen eyes, Naldo tried to read the paper Salazar left for him. His vision was a total blur.

Cruz entered and Naldo thrust the paper at him. "What about 'em?" Cruz asked after reading it.

"He wants 'em gone. All of 'em! He thinks they're cuttin' into his territory."

"Really?" Cruz asked, skeptical.

"What the fuck did you just say?" Cruz instantly froze and put his head down.

"You and Bosco check it out. Then call Vasquez and get his guys over. Tell Big Frankie to call his uncle. I need to get this done."

Their target was a dilapidated, run-down house tucked away at the end of a desolate alley. The only signs of life were the flickering lights from inside and the muffled sound of voices. As they approached, they could see shadows moving about through the dirty windows, indicating a hive of activity inside. Fifteen punks scurried around, their hands busy with separating and packaging drugs in various corners of the house and garage. The stench of chemicals hung heavy in the air, mixing with the acrid smell of smoke and sweat. In one corner, the lead punk stood over his girlfriend, testing their latest batch by shoving it up her nose without a second thought. Clearly this was prime shit based upon her reaction.

Cruz and two dozen armed bangers fanned out down the alley toward the drug house.

At the same time, the quiet hum of a dark SUV filled the air as it made its way down the street perpendicular to the alley, a family of five inside. The father sat behind the wheel, his hands gripped tightly on the steering wheel while the mother was in the passenger seat. In the back, three young children played and giggled, their ages ranging from 2 to 5 years old. Two girls and one boy. The youngest, a baby secured in an infant car seat, slept peacefully.

The robotic voice of the car's GPS then instructed them to "Turn right ahead." The husband obediently turned into the narrow alley, unsure of where it would lead. As they drove further in, all he could see was a half-painted over sign that read "Through Street" instead of the usual warning of "Not a Through Street". The walls on either side were adorned with layers of graffiti, ranging from playful doodles to crude statements and everything in between. However, one particular piece caught his eye — a menacing phrase painted in large drippy red letters: *Avenida Asesinos*, which translated to *Assassin Avenue*. Suddenly, the once mundane alley held an air of danger.

"Honey, this doesn't look right," said the mother.

As Cruz' men neared the house, they heard the car coming up behind them. One of Cruz' guys accidentally knocked over a trash can. Floodlights instantly illuminated the drug house and sent Cruz' men into a frenzy.

In quick succession, the driver of the SUV realized he couldn't get through while the drug house punks poured out, wielding guns. He frantically attempted a U-turn, but before he could fully maneuver his vehicle, a swarm of Cruz' men descended upon them, unleashing a storm of gunfire. The drug house punks, caught off guard but not unprepared, fired back at their attackers. The air was thick with the deafening sound of gunshots as both sides exchanged fire relentlessly. A mini war zone of crossfire with casualties piling up on both sides.

With a roar of the engine, the driver slammed his foot down on the accelerator just before being shot. His wife crawled into the back of the SUV. A bullet pierced through the windshield, hitting her in the neck and grazing her head. Blood sprayed everywhere, splattering on the baby and covering the 3-year-old's head in a crimson mask. The child slumped over, her body limp and lifeless. The third child, only slightly injured from a ricochet, was covered in blood spatter and crying uncontrollably in fear and confusion. As the SUV careened out of the alley and onto the street, its metal exterior riddled with bullet holes, it crashed into a utility pole with a deafening crunch. Shards of glass and twisted metal scattered across the road, creating a chaotic scene amidst the gunshots and screams.

A loud BOOM shook the walls of the drug house, causing broken glass and other debris to scatter in every direction. Cruz' few remaining men frantically searched for an escape route as police sirens wailed in the distance, growing closer by the second. Their hearts raced with a mix of fear and adrenaline as they scrambled to flee before getting caught and facing either a lifetime behind bars or Naldo's ruthless retribution.

CHAPTER SEVEN
WAR BEGINS

The next day's newspaper headline screamed out in stark black letters:

Gang War Erupts: FAMILY ATTACKED,
BABY KILLED.

The accompanying photo showed a grim-faced Mayor with another story to the right of it: *"Mayor On Firing Line To Take Action."*

Police cars formed a barricade at the entrance to the notorious alley as officers scoured the area for evidence, their eyes trained on every inch of the road leading to the drug house, now a charred skeleton with three fire trucks parked in front. Forensic detectives zipped up body bags as cops marked hundreds of spent cartridges.

Back at the entrance to the alley, an elderly woman with weathered hands gently placed flowers into a small hole in the wall, just above the graffiti that read "Avenida Asesinos". Her grief was palpable, a stark contrast to the ruthless gang violence that had claimed yet another innocent life.

A female reporter stood in front of the camera, accompanied by her cameraman who was busy capturing footage. She confidently reported, "I talked to dozens of people who live in this neighborhood and the sentiment was the same... that instead of cleaning up the gangs on this street, the police simply ignored it." Behind her, a group of kids gathered, flashing gang hand signals to the news camera and giggling. "Stay tuned to this station for our eleven o'clock special tonight, *Dead End Murders*."

That night, the broadcast went national. On the main monitor inside a TV studio, a New York reporter came up live. "This is Joseph Gonzalez in New York for K-News at 11. People here are reacting as if they've lost one of their own. These were just a few scenes in Jamaica earlier today." The video showed a group of citizens beating up four gangbangers near a housing project, followed by a citizen with a baseball bat running past the camera after a gangbanger with facial tattoos.

"And stay the hell out of this neighborhood," yelled the citizen vigilante.

Gonzalez continued, "And we see this happening all over the country."

He was right. It was the same in every city. Citizens everywhere were fed up and not going to take it anymore. Gangbangers were being chased and attacked, beaten with sticks, baseball bats, bricks, whatever the vigilantes could get their hands on. One old man gardener in Detroit was whacking a young, heavily tattooed thug with his shovel after he discovered him ripping up his tomato plants. This was war, now on the citizens' terms.

The day of Marco's funeral had finally arrived, a somber event that the Lorenzo family had been dreading. Despite their tribulation, they were fortunate to have Marco's body back in their possession. Naldo, with a twisted sense of humor, had dumped it onto the dry concrete bed of the L.A. River, with a smiley-face balloon attached. After the authorities completed their investigation and followed through with necessary protocols, including an autopsy, Marco's lifeless body was finally released back to his father.

A small group of Lorenzo family members gathered at the grave site, where a priest offered words of comfort to Mr.

Lorenzo and Grandma. It was the second funeral Rico had attended in a short period of time, adding to his already heavy heart. He approached the grave site but remained at a distance, unsure how he would be received by the rest of the family. Mr. Lorenzo spotted Rico but couldn't bring himself to look at him, overwhelmed with grief and anger about his son.

Rico stayed. The priest finished. The family moved toward each other, toward the casket, toward whatever came next. One by one they filtered away until Rico was the only one still standing there, hat in his hands, alone at the edge of the grave. He made the sign of the cross then walked to his car.

Back at the entrance to the dead-end alley, dozens of parents with their children carried signs that read: "Stop the Slaughter Now", "Save Our Children" and "No More!" They were walking in a circle and chanting repeatedly: "No More Violence. No More Violence." The previously graffitied wall had been covered up with fresh paint, but one word stood out in bright yellow —— "COWARDS!" Along the surrounding fences and walls, there were hundreds of memorial flowers laid out in remembrance.

A sleek, black limo pulled up to the curb and Mayor Grayson emerged from the door, flanked by his stern-faced bodyguards. As soon as his feet hit the pavement, a swarm of reporters and concerned citizens surrounded him. The flashing lights of cameras captured every movement as he made his way towards the alley. Suddenly, a Latina woman burst through the crowd, her eyes wild with anger as she shoved a picture of her toddler son into Grayson's face. "They killed my baby last year," she screamed, her voice raw with emotion. "Where were you then?"

The bodyguards quickly intervened, attempting to ease her away from the mayor, but she collapsed to the ground in anguish. Without hesitation, Mayor Grayson extended a hand to help her up and took the photo from her trembling hands. He studied it for a moment before turning to face the cameras.

"You all have every right to be angry," he announced solemnly. "Our children deserve to be protected at all costs. They rely on us and we cannot...we will not...let them down again." His arm instinctively wrapped around the distraught mother's shoulder, offering what little comfort he could. "Starting today, I am ordering increased police patrols in this alley. And anyone caught..."

Before he could finish his statement, an angry voice rose from the crowd. "It's not enough!" a woman shouted. "What about all the other alleys and streets?"

The crowd picked up its chants again. "It's not enough. It's not enough." Grayson couldn't get a word in edgewise.

As the sun set on the quiet neighborhood, a stream of neighbors made their way towards a corner house not too far from the dead-end alley. Plates of food were carried by some of the women, while others chattered solemnly amongst themselves. Inside, the sound of loud conversations spilled out onto the streets, as dozens more men and women had already gathered for this important meeting.

In the center of it all stood Councilman Rico, looking tired and weighed down by the burden he carried. He raised his hands for silence and spoke with a determined strength in his voice. "No one person, no one group can be expected to fight the gangs and end the crime. This is something we must all do together to make a lasting difference. It's time we take back our neighborhoods."

The crowd erupted in agreement, shouting "Si! Together! Right!" Then the room went quiet again and a heavyset woman in the back raised her hand. She didn't wait to be called on. "I run the laundromat on Cesar Chavez. Three times they came in. Three times." She held up her fingers so no one could miss it. "Last time they pistol-whipped my nephew because he wouldn't hand over the cash fast enough. He's seventeen. Still can't hear right out of one ear." She lowered her hand and looked straight at Rico. "I'm done waiting for somebody else to fix this."

A murmur of recognition moved through the room — people nodding, exchanging glances, some looking at the floor because they had their own version of the same story. An older man near the window said quietly, "My grandson won't walk to school anymore. Takes the bus two extra stops just to avoid one block." Nobody laughed. Nobody had to.

One by one others stepped forward. A young mother whose daughter had stopped playing outside. A shop owner who'd started sleeping in his storeroom to protect his inventory. A retired teacher who recognized three of the kids in the alley shooting footage from her own classroom. Rico listened to all of it. He didn't check his watch. He didn't interrupt. By the time the last person spoke, the plates of food sat mostly untouched and the room had gone from grief to something harder and more useful.

On another night, at a neighborhood sports bar, Rico was alone at a table in back quietly nursing a drink. TV sets were all tuned to the same station and some of the bar's customers watched a *Coop Cooper Town Hall Event*.

In a TV studio, Coop Cooper, a dapper 50-year old, was interviewing six gangbangers in New York City who were wearing bandannas that covered the lower halves of their faces. "You can't tell me that what happened in that alley doesn't bother you guys," Coop said. "After all we're talking about killing babies here."

"Hey, man," said the lead banger. "I don't wanna speak for our Angeleno brothers but defending our turf..."

A middle-aged Black woman from the TV audience ran up to the stage, frothing with anger, and shook her finger in the banger's face. "Who the hell do you think you are... all of you are nothing but cowards. My son was killed by punks like you. Talking about your turf... your turf... like you're some kinda kings or something." The TV audience reacted loudly and cheered the woman on.

Rico saw more and more people in the bar start to pay attention to the show. They nodded in agreement with the woman on TV with some calling out the gangbangers as 'fucking lowlifes'.

The bangers on the TV stage shifted in their seats uncomfortably, screaming at the audience to "shut the fuck up" and hurling racial and other vile insults. The audience came right back at them. Coop tried to take control of the situation. "Hold on a minute. Hold on." Then his words shifted directly to the lead banger. "So do you have anything to say to this woman who lost her son?" The Black woman stood on stage shaking, ready to explode.

"Maybe he was in the wrong place at the wrong time. You take your chances," said the same banger.

"Take your chances? How about you take your chances right now, asshole?" The Black woman lunged forward and ripped the bandana off the banger's face. The other bangers reacted by rushing towards her, causing the studio's security guards to intervene and push them back. It was bordering on a melee.

Rico scanned the boisterous crowd in the sports bar, all rooting for the Black woman on TV. He chugged the last of his drink and headed out.

At a nighttime ShowGun location shoot, the same film director and crew seen working with Mair previously were preparing a scene with actors posing as two veteran detectives in their 40s and three punks in their 20s.

"Let's do another run through," said the director. "Nick, just as you pass the swings, I want you to turn around and fire another shot. Okay, everyone, standby."

Mair and George, serving as gun wranglers for this scene, were standing near the camera operator as the director took his position at the monitor. "Okay, Action!"

The "Detectives" chased the "Punks" across a playground and gunfire was exchanged. Suddenly behind the action, two explosions and a huge fireball lit the sky. From everyone's reaction, it was apparent it was not part of the scene.

"Cut! Cut! What the hell was that?"

As chaos erupted on set, Mair and George sprang into action, racing towards where they knew their ShowGun trucks were parked. But when they arrived, all of their worst fears were confirmed. Both trucks were engulfed in flames, sending thick black smoke billowing into the sky. Other members of the film crew rushed in, but there was nothing anyone could do except watch helplessly as everything they had worked so hard for went up in flames.

Moments later, Rico's phone rang in his quiet home where he had been lounging barefoot on his couch, reading a book, dressed only in a tee-shirt and sweats. He answered to hear Mair's frantic voice screaming, "They blew up my trucks! Get out of there!" He was already moving before she finished the sentence — off the couch, across the floor, out the front door — and he had just cleared the porch steps when the back of the house blew. The force of it lifted him off his feet and slammed him onto the front lawn, the heat rolling over him in a single searing wave. He lay there a moment, ears ringing, face pressed against the grass, before he pushed himself up onto his hands and knees. By the time dawn broke, the once beautiful home was now burned and charred, still smoldering as firefighters poked through the wreckage. Rico sat on the curb, his face expressionless, as he clutched Dolores' small music box in his hands.

CHAPTER EIGHT

RETRIBUTION

The music box had wound down, but Rico hadn't moved. A woman came out from the house next door, stepped past the yellow tape, and set a cup of coffee and a plate of food on the curb beside him without a word. He didn't touch it.

From his top-floor office at GangBanger Central, Naldo peered through the smudged window and watched the activity below. The deafening sounds of metal tearing apart filled the air as workers dismantled cars with precision and speed. Some men inside the cars looked like they were just going through the motion of doing their jobs. Each one, though, kept a keen eye on Naldo or the door, knowing that something big was about to go down. Big Frankie and Cruz seemed especially anxious.

The same armed men and more, belonging to Salazar, stood tall and vigilant, weapons at the ready, positioned in the same spots as they had been during Salazar's previous visit.

And then Salazar himself entered, flanked by his two heavily armed bodyguards. He wasted no time in surveying the activity within the warehouse, his sharp eyes taking it all in as he moved across the floor.

With a flick of a switch, Naldo unleashed a deafening blast of rap music that echoed through the warehouse. It served as a signal to his well-coordinated men, who sprang into action with an assault against Salazar's henchmen.

Grinder Man wielded his powerful grinder like a weapon, nearly decapitating one of the armed guards in a single swift motion. Drill Guy followed suit, shoving his electric drill into the back of another guard with such force that he splintered the man's spine. Painter Guy emerged with his paint gun and shot a thick stream of shiny black goo into the face of a different guard while a second guy bashed him in the head with a tire iron. Big Frankie, with his massive strength and size, swung a hanging engine down onto the head of still another guard, crushing the man's skull under its weight.

When one of Salazar's bodyguards swung his gun toward Naldo and fired, the shot punched into the wall behind him. Big Frankie pushed a shop cooling fan with exposed blades into him. The bodyguard was neatly sliced and diced. Cruz and other workers descended on Salazar's remaining guards like cockroaches. They stabbed them with screwdrivers and bludgeoned them with hammers and tire irons.

Everything was happening lightning fast. Salazar spun in terror and confusion, not knowing which way to run until he attempted to flee… right up the steep stairs to Naldo's office. He was met by Naldo who stood at the top blocking his escape. From his higher position, Naldo swung his leg up and kicked Salazar hard in the face causing him to tumble down backwards and land in a crumpled heap at the bottom of the steps.

Naldo then descended slowly and stood over the bleeding, half-conscious drug kingpin. "You think you can come into my city, yeah, that's right, *my* city, and put your hands on me? You think I'd let you do that again?"

"Give him a beat down, Naldo, like he gave you," said Cruz. Naldo shot Cruz a dirty look for reminding him.

"Do him, Naldo," urged Big Frankie.

Naldo's eyes scanned the faces of his men, watching their reactions with a smug satisfaction. They were goading him on, urging him to take action. As he turned to Salazar, his voice dripped with menace. "You ever want something from me, you better ask nice. You come up here and threaten me again and I'll make sure it takes a fucking year for you to die." Naldo wasn't being magnanimous; he was being strategic. He knew that any retaliation from Salazar's associates could draw unwanted attention and cause trouble for his operation.

Turning to Cruz, he barked out an order. "Get him the fuck outta here." And then, with a nod towards Big Frankie, he added, "And you...clean up this mess."

Cruz grunted and strained, his muscles bulging as he tried to hoist the heavy Salazar off the floor but he couldn't budge him. Naldo screamed out to another worker, "Well, help him, ya lazy fuck!" The worker jumped in to help Cruz and together they managed to half-lift and half-drag Salazar away from the bloody scene.

Big Frankie's eyes scanned the floor filled with bodies and body parts — an ear here, a nose there, the occasional head, arm, hand and garbled mass of guts — not knowing where to start on the gruesome mess. He watched as one younger worker puked uncontrollably in a corner.

Naldo then added, "Then pack up. We're outta here."

The stench of blood and death hung heavily in the air, mixed with oil, paint and gunpowder.

Rico was now staying in a hotel room and wearing the same clothes he had on during the firebombing of his home. From the hotel window, he could see the glittering lights of the city, a stark contrast to the darkness and chaos he had just left behind. But Rico wasn't ready for anything bright in his life just yet; he reached up and pulled the curtains closed then retreated to bed.

Much later, the sound of knocking on the door increased to pounding. There was movement amid the darkness as Rico, looking like he just woke up, opened the door to Councilwoman Park. She walked past him into the room. "You stink. You need to get cleaned up." She drew back the curtains to let in some light and air out the room.

"I decided I need to be away for awhile," said Rico.

"You might want to rethink that after you hear what I have to say."

He rummaged through one of two shopping bags on the floor and pulled out toothpaste and a brush then went into the adjoining bathroom and half-closed the door.

Park stood just outside, leaning against the wall where she couldn't see in. "The police looked but can't find anybody. It's as if the gangs have all disappeared. This could be our chance to accomplish community out-reach... without any interference from them."

Rico came back into the room. "The only thing I've been good at accomplishing is getting my daughter and friend's son killed and another friend's business destroyed."

He went to the door and opened it for her to leave. It wasn't like him to be so abrupt but Park understood — he just wasn't ready. Still, she hoped he'd change his mind. She stood still a moment then said, "I'm sorry, Javier," as she sadly walked out.

Days had passed since Rico had last stepped foot outside. With a heavy heart, he made his way to the cemetery and knelt before Dolores' grave. The morning air was cool and still, with only a few birds singing in the distance. As he finished his prayers, he made the sign of the cross and rose to his feet. He carefully placed a single white rose on top of the gravestone as he whispered words of love and farewell. Just as he was about to turn away, a loud buzzing caught his attention. A wasp had landed on the rose, its black and yellow striped body sharp against the pale petals. Instinctively, Rico brushed it away with a quick movement of his hand. The wasp flew off, but Rico's eyes followed it until it disappeared up into a nearby tree where he could see a large nest tucked among the branches.

This led him back to Mair and the ShowGun Warehouse. As he walked by the charred remains of ShowGun trucks, he heard George's and Mair's voices echoing from inside the warehouse.

"Mair!" George's voice was strained, as if trying to quell a raging storm.

"What about the trucks?" Mair's voice echoed through the walls, filled with frustration and anger.

"They can be replaced too."

"It was my *first* truck!" she said furiously.

Inside, George and others were sifting through salvaged equipment, examining each piece carefully. Mair stood in the center of it all, visibly upset as she slammed a charred rifle onto the concrete floor. She looked as though she were ready to tear her hair out in frustration. But then, George wheeled himself over and picked up the damaged weapon.

Rico stepped into the warehouse, his expression heavy with guilt. "I just stopped by to tell you how sorry I am for getting you mixed up in my business."

Mair and George turned to face him, their expressions filled with surprise. Mair took a deep breath before responding. "It was my decision. And besides, this is everyone's business now. I just need some time to be upset."

"I think I have a way to make this right," Rico declared, determination glimmering in his eyes. "I started this fight and now I'm going to finish it."

Rico turned to walk away but Mair's sharp tone stopped him in his tracks. "You're not going anywhere until you tell me what's going on."

Rico hesitated, knowing that this would only cause more pain for Mair. "This has been too hard on you already."

"Javier!" Her sharp tone cut through the air, demanding an explanation.

He relented and began to explain his plan. "We've been doing it all wrong. The way to stop the gangs permanently is to take out the nest."

"The nest?" George echoed, confused by the new terminology. Mair looked equally puzzled.

"We can't take them out one at a time. We need to hit them all at the same time, at their stronghold — the Alamo."

"From what I heard, the place is a fucking fortress," George said.

"The only reason it hasn't been tried is because no one wants another Waco or Ruby Ridge," added Rico.

"The Alamo. Just the name…" Mair shuddered, remembering the infamous battle that took place there.

"With a good team and strategic planning, we can take them down like we did with Al Qaeda," Rico said confidently. "Destroy their infrastructure and gather as much info on their network. And, we have the momentum."

"How's that?" asked George.

"Maybe," said Mair, her mind already racing with possibilities.

"People are fed up. If we clean up the Alamo, we win. If there are any repercussions, the whole country will be behind us."

George reasoned, "He's right. We win either way."

Mair paced as she thought. She spotted Dolores' wedding invitation and photos of her military team then turned back to Rico. "You're a councilman now."

"The people who wage wars ought to be willing to fight them," he said. "Now, what are we going to do about guns? I doubt Morrison can get any and I know Mark can't."

"Follow me." Mair and George led Rico to a special locked room. When she opened the door, she said "Welcome to the war room." The walls were filled with posters from war movies from World War I through the latest and it was filled with hundreds of heavy-duty weaponry.

"All we have to do is convert them back into the real thing and function test the shit out of them with live ammo," said George.

"We'll need a logistics expert," said Rico. He and Mair both looked at George. "We said we'd find something for you."

"I'm up for it... so to speak."

"I'll call Morrison and Jamieson and see how many men they can come up with," said Rico. "Now, we just need someone who can blow shit up." All three exchanged looks, each one understanding what the other was thinking.

Days later, George, Morrison and Bobby made their way through the raucous Queen Mary nightclub, a place made famous for its female impersonators. The place was filled with patrons of every persuasion, some dressed to the nines. A large group of older folks who obviously escaped their senior care facility were at one table while it looked like it was a fun night out for a ladies book club at another. "I don't believe this," muttered Bobby who wore middle-grade denim and a sandy pink pullover. "How come no one told me?" He now regretted his color choice.

A wiry 45-year-old guy named Schizwicki in a black leather motorcycle jacket with silver studs sat at a far table. George caught sight of him and wheeled ahead of Morrison and Bobby. On the way, he stopped a waitress. "Four beers. Over there. Thanks." He then shouted out, "Hey, Schizwicki, how's it hangin?"

Bobby turned to Morrison. "Did he just say that?" Morrison laughed loudly. "Who *is* this guy?" Bobby asked.

"Best explosives expert we know.

"No fucking way."

"Force Recon. Until they found out about his... hobby."

"You mean he's —"

"— He ain't gay, if that's what you were about to say."

"I don't get it."

The men sat at Schizwicki's table as the waitress served up the beers.

"Hey, Schiz," said Morrison.

"Long time no see," answered Schiz.

Bobby muttered under his breath, "Wonder why," as he swiveled uncomfortably in his seat to make himself invisible.

"Matthew J. Schizwicki, I'd like you to meet Bobby Lopez," said Morrison.

"How are ya?"

Bobby looked around nervously. "Okay."

"He thought we were going on a tour of a ship," said George who chuckled.

Schizwicki laughed.

"So, what do you think?" Morrison asked.

"Hell yeah. I could use the practice. Besides, Rico did me a solid back in the day."

Morrison turned to Bobby as if to say *I told ya,* which of course he hadn't.

"It'll be fun. Hey, I gotta go get ready. Enjoy the show." Schizwicki got up and headed to the dressing room.

"Oh, jeez, you gotta be kidding," said Bobby. "We're not actually staying for this, are we?" George and Morrison smiled, hanged back and drank their beers while Bobby squirmed.

Rico's plan was coming together. Within the week, a special shooting session had been arranged to test fire the newly configured weapons. Laid out on benches at an outdoor shooting range were handguns, shotguns, sub-machine guns and sniper rifles. Rico, Mair, Bobby, Morrison, Jamieson and many of the same men who volunteered for previous missions all stood at the ready facing downrange. George was off to the side acting as safety range officer while Mair was at the far left with a sniper rifle and on the far right were Morrison's men, three were snipers. Everyone else was in between.

Morrison turned to Rico. "So, you think you still got it?"

"We'll see."

George announced, "All clear down range. Commence firing."

The barrage began as all fired away. Rico and Morrison shot rifles. Jamison and Bobby were using MP5s and P-90 sub-machine guns.

The action then slowed and some of them stopped firing.

"Cease Fire!" said George. "All clear?"

The shooters unloaded their weapons and placed them on the benches. After doing so, everyone answered in the affirmative.

Morrison glanced at Rico's targets and saw good groupings. "Not bad if I say so myself," said Rico. What distance were *your* guys shooting?"

"500 yards."

Rico moved to Morrison's spotting scope. He peered through and saw a group of bullet holes the size of a half-dollar in each of the snipers' targets. He then peered over to Mair's target. It was blank. "She must be having a bad day."

"Really?" said Morrison. He stepped in and looked through the scope then tilted it up to see the farther targets. "Ahhh. That's my girl."

Mair put her rifle away, not really paying attention to Rico, Morrison and the snipers who gathered around them.

"Check the 800 yard target," said Morrison.

Mair's target showed another half-dollar-sized grouping. Wilson, the main sniper, looked over at Mair, impressed, while others took turns looking through the scope. They were all equally in awe.

Mair then turned to George. "George, your turn."

"And hurry it up. We don't have all day," joked Morrison.

Mair gave George an MP5 as he wheeled himself into position facing a target 25-yards downrange. He obliterated it. "Fast enough for you?" George asked Morrison with his cocksure smile. They both laughed.

With their refresher target practice and weapons-testing completed, Rico's plan unfolded in rapid order.

Outside ShowGun's warehouse, George oversaw men loading guns and equipment into an RV, four SUVs and a truck. "Make sure the shields for the windows are in the truck."

Jamieson pulled up in a van and opened the side door just as Rico and Mair exited the warehouse.

"Your stuff will go into the truck," Rico said to Jamieson.

"I got us a little extra insurance if you want it." Jamieson slid back the top of a large box, revealing the contents to Rico and Mair. Their eyes popped.

"Jesus. Does it work?" Mair asked.

Jamieson shrugged nonchalantly. "Hell if I know."

"Then we'd better take a pass." Without another word, Rico disappeared into the warehouse.

"What a shame. I was hoping you'd have ammo for it."

George wheeled over to the open box and peered inside, his face lighting up with excitement. "Let me see what I can find."

"Looks good to me. Load it anyway," said Mair. "We have room."

Morrison called out to Mair from inside the warehouse. "Mair, got a question." She headed back in and saw Bobby closing up one of the safes. Jamieson then came in.

"You got all the prop guns put away?" Mair asked, raising her voice to be heard over the activity.

"Yeah that's all we need... going in shooting blanks," said Jamieson with a smirk.

"I'm not *that* stupid," said Bobby as he turned to face them..

A new voice sounded from the open door, causing everyone to turn and look. Tanaka stood there, a large duffel bag slung over one shoulder. He surveyed the scene before him with a critical eye. " So how stupid are you?" he asked pointedly, raising an eyebrow at Bobby's comment.

Bobby rolled his eyes and let out an exasperated sigh. "Nice to see you too," he muttered under his breath.

Rico stepped forward, breaking the tension. "Hey everybody," he said with a warm smile. "Michael Tanaka."

Tanaka nodded in acknowledgement to the group before turning to Mair. She gestured towards a nearby worktable. "You can put your stuff over there," she said politely.

But Tanaka's attention was already focused on Morrison, who was now walking towards them. The two men greeted each other warmly, shaking hands and exchanging some quick pleasantries.

Wilson entered with his rifle case and ammo boxes while sounds of a muscle car rumbled outside. A moment later, Schizwicki, now with black earring studs and the same black leather jacket, entered. He was carrying a large box of explosives under each arm.

Jamieson shouted, "Hey, Schizwicki! Bobby, give him a hand."

Bobby was still a bit taken aback by Schizwicki's appearance but he ran over and took one of the boxes and put it on a table.

"I wish I could have gotten more remote detonators," said Schizwicki.

"Then why didn't you?" asked Bobby.

Schizwicki leaned in close to him. "Cause they don't stock them at Home Depot, dipshit."

Morrison and his men shook their heads and laughed as Schizwicki turned and walked off. "Anyway, I got the timers for the first group." He then turned back to Bobby. "And you, kid, can help me cut fuses." Schizwicki then crossed paths with Tanaka. They stopped and eyed each other for a long moment — two volatile men with a history.

"Hey," said Schizwicki.

"Hey," said Tanaka.

They then went their separate ways.

Rico scanned the activity and saw Mair packing her gear. He walked over and put his hand on her shoulder. She turned and saw a concerned look in his eyes. "I'm going," she said forcefully.

Just then, George yelled out, "Hey Jamie! I found what you need and lots of it."

"I can't lose you too," Rico told Mair. That hit her, but in a good way. "I know you can shoot…"

Mair reassured him. "I never planned on going in."

"Oh."

"I'll hang back with Wilson."

Relieved, Rico took a breath. "That's what I was going to suggest."

Mair's look expressed – *yeah right!* She knew Rico wasn't quite as progressive as he made himself out to be when it came to certain subjects.

Rico quickly turned to the group and held up a thumb drive. "I have the aerials."

CHAPTER NINE
THE ALAMO

Everyone, except Rico, was dressed in black or dark camouflage. Rico wore casual clothes and a bright yellow windbreaker. The group loaded themselves into the vehicles and drove off — widely separated, surface streets to freeways to rural roadways, nothing that looked like a convoy to anyone who might be watching.

It was late afternoon when they arrived at a secure location overlooking the Alamo. The teams made final preparations, and a drone was being unpacked while Mair and Wilson set up sniper positions.

Jamieson grabbed a bunch of earpieces and tossed packs to Morrison then helped distribute the devices to the rest of the men.

Morrison grabbed a pair of binoculars. "I'm gonna have a look-see," he said as he walked off.

Jamieson took a small surveillance pin in the shape of the American flag from the box and made a few minor adjustments to it. "Hey Rico." Rico walked over and Jamieson tacked the pin to his collar.

Schizwicki was off to the side. He took off his shirt to put on a ballistic vest. A tattoo on his chest — a heart with the initials "D.F." inside it for Delta Force. And one more thing; he was wearing a woman's laced corset. He strapped the vest on over it.

Bobby was in shock. "What the fuck are you doing?" Schizwicki glared at him and the other men took notice. "I mean if they catch you, you know what they'll do to you?"

Schizwicki said nothing. He calmly pulled his shirt back on and went back to strapping on his gear. A beat passed. Then another. Still not looking at Bobby, he said, "Have you ever seen lions hunt? It's the females that do all the killing. They're strong, they're quick and they get the job done. This belonged to my mother. She was a fucking lion." Not another word from Bobby. He turned back to what he had been doing as did the other men.

Morrison strode back to the group, his face grave as he approached Rico. "We might have a problem."

"What do you mean?"

"How old are those aerials?"

Jamieson overheard and joined them as he waved over Tanaka. "Some of the stuff down there isn't on the aerials," said Morrison.

Rico gestured for him to lead the way. "Show me."

The four of them made their way to the concealed area where Morrison had conducted his recon. The group went prone and Rico and Jamieson peered through their binoculars, scanning the terrain below.

"They've been busy," said Rico. "What do you think?"

Jamieson studied the scene carefully before responding, "Definitely different. But I think we can still pull it off." He then passed his binoculars to Tanaka.

Tanaka took his time. He scanned left, then right, then back to center. "More turf, more exposure. They got greedy. That works for us."

Rico's gaze shifted from Jamieson to Morrison and finally rested on Tanaka. "Agreed," Morrison stated firmly.

"The opportunity of defeating the enemy is provided by the enemy himself," quoted Rico, a hint of admiration in his voice.

"You're quoting Sun Tzu now?" Tanaka asked.

"I give credit where credit is due."

They all walked back to the main staging area then Rico, Morrison and Jamieson went over to one of the SUVs where one of Jamieson's men was holding his tool bag as he closed the trunk. "Ready?" asked Jamieson.

The man walked around to the front of the SUV and lowered the hood. "She's good to go," he said, giving the hood a pat.

Morrison patted Rico on the back and walked off. "I'll tell George and the others."

Meanwhile, Jamieson stepped forward and began pointing out various parts of the SUV to Rico. "We have a camera here, another one here and here," he said, gesturing to different areas. "There's a microphone here and here, and we've also installed an extra battery and signal booster for the earpieces."

Rico nodded. "From what we've seen, I think if it's parked with the rest of their vehicles, we should have some good visuals and audio." He checked his watch then looked over to Mair who had been watching him. They walked towards each other. No embrace, no handshake, just an intense moment. "Thank you for always being there," he said.

"Be safe."

"You too," said Rico. He turned and headed back to the SUV, climbing inside as Jamieson gave him a final word of encouragement. "See you on the other side," he said, "Good luck."

Mair watched Rico drive off.

The abandoned steel mill known as the Alamo stood in ruins, with collapsed buildings and walls crumbling under the weight of time. Chunks and slabs of concrete lay scattered around twisted steel girders, a chaotic landscape frozen in decay. The once bustling compound now housed makeshift living quarters within old shipping containers, their rusted exteriors blending into the industrial surroundings. Enveloping it all was a fortified fence, lined with menacing coils of razor wire and other deadly obstacles. Makeshift alarms, fashioned out of anything that could make noise, encircled the perimeter like a chorus of warning sirens. The atmosphere was tense and foreboding, with danger lurking behind every corner of this forgotten place.

As Rico's car approached the entrance, a stark white flag flapped proudly from the antenna. Perched atop the crumbling wall was a lone gunman, his weapon trained on the vehicle. One by one, more armed men emerged, their eyes scanning for any signs of threat. Rico exited his car with his hands raised. "I'm unarmed," he called out to them.

One of the armed men quickly dialed a number on his cell phone, and after a tense few minutes, the rusty gate creaked open. Stepping through were Naldo, Big Frankie, and Cruz, along with a few other familiar faces from the warehouse. Their eyes scanned Rico cautiously, but when they saw his unarmed state and the white flag waving from his car, they relaxed slightly.

"Still alive and kicking, I see. You got some big balls coming here by yourself," said Naldo. "No one gets in unless they're from the streets."

Rico nonchalantly undid the buttons of his shirt, revealing a tapestry of street tattoos that covered his chest. Naldo couldn't help but laugh at the sight. However, before he could say anything else, a large rock slammed into Rico's broad chest, knocking him to his knees. Naldo whipped around to see Rooster, a comical little runt with fiery orange hair and a noticeable lisp, jumping up and down in hysterics. "Get him the fuck outta here," ordered Naldo. Two bangers quickly dragged Rooster off as Rico stood back up, brushing off dirt and debris from his knees.

"It's not going to be that easy," Naldo said. He then motioned to Big Frankie who walked forward and patted Rico down for any weapons or surveillance devices.

"I just want to talk," said Rico, as he was being pounded by Big Frankie's platter-sized hands.

Naldo surveyed the area and shrugged, knowing he had the upper hand either way. He and Big Frankie escorted the councilman through the gates while Cruz jumped into Rico's SUV.

The camp was teeming with activity. Armed men were everywhere. Others ate, slept or worked at their assigned duties. "Welcome to the house that Naldo built!" The sound echoed through the air, a testament to the strength and power of its owner. Rico couldn't help but feel both intimidated and in awe of the scene before him.

Naldo's men smirked as Rico was led past a camouflaged area filled with vehicles, gaudily painted vans, motorcycles, some hot cars. Nearby were a gas pump, fuel trucks and gas tanks. Cruz drove Rico's SUV in to become part of the line-up. "I need a few things," Cruz told Naldo as he thumped the SUV's dashboard.

"Take what you want." Then to Rico, Naldo said, "As you might have guessed... transportation department. By the way, this is just the Latinos' turf." A few others emerged from the shadows to join Big Frankie and Naldo as they escorted Rico.

"There..." Naldo pointed far to the left, "... the Gringos." Then he pointed to two more areas off right, "Black Brothers... Asian Brothers. They got their own. But mine's the best." Naldo's chest puffed out with pride as he surveyed his domain. "And in case you didn't notice... no tagging. This is neutral ground."

They continued on, past a vegetable garden, with a pumpkin patch and a power plant with generators humming. "Fresh veggies," Naldo continued. "We had a bomb

Thanksgiving with our turkey and punk-in pies." Rico couldn't help but notice the familiar speech pattern in Naldo's words — *'turkey and punk-in pies'* — and now realized that Naldo was Marco's killer. His jaw tightened. His eyes went flat. He held the breath in his chest.

Naldo then opened the heavy doors to a vast room filled with shelves upon shelves of canned food and supplies. He threw open his arms and proclaimed. "Two fucking years. That's how long we can last."

After that, they came upon another camouflaged area where heavily tattooed women watched Rico suspiciously as they cooked. Naldo pointed to a different area. "Future Day Care over there." Rico looked surprised. "You see, we're always thinking," Naldo continued. "Something you don't think we ever do. When our kids grow, they'll be stronger and more organized. Just like the church, we'll start 'em early." The more Rico saw, the more he was stunned by the scope of it all. He was just thankful there weren't any kids being harbored there yet.

Naldo then escorted Rico into a building made from multiple shipping containers. The walls were lined with desks and computer stations, manned by a diligent staff of his followers. Naldo gestured proudly to the high-tech equipment surrounding them. "State of the art," he boasted, placing his hand on top of a sleek backup drive. "Even our own backup."

He turned to one of his computer experts and asked, "What do you call this thing again?"

"A backup drive?" replied the technician, unsure if it was a trick question.

Naldo let out a strained chuckle. "That's funny," he said through gritted teeth.

Another computer guy waved at Naldo to get his attention. Naldo went over to him as the guy pointed to his computer screen. "You tell him the price is the price," said Naldo. "No fuckin' discounts this time." The technician nodded and began typing away.

Naldo saw Rico focused on the computers. "Dope, isn't it?" he said. Rico took a mental inventory as Naldo led him out.

There was one last stop on Naldo's little tour. Two huge guards pulled open two metal vault doors at their final destination — the arsenal. "The sugar on the churro. I got so many buyers lined up for this shit. Pretty soon I'll be taking away customers from the Feds." Rico tried to hide his shock at the sheer quantity and variety of arms before him that were stacked on shelves and in dozens of boxes.

Meanwhile, high above the Alamo in their RV lookout, Morrison, Jamieson, Tanaka, and George huddled around surveillance monitors displaying footage from three different angles: two from the SUV's cameras and one from Rico's discreetly placed flag pin camera.

"Fuck, they got RPGs?" said an astounded Morrison.

"George, you got this marked on the layout?" Jamieson asked.

"I mapped out everything Rico saw from the time he entered."

They saw Naldo's men push the vault door closed. "I came to negotiate a truce," said Rico. "The killing has to stop."

"Shut up. You'll get your chance. This is my time."

Rico started to speak again but Naldo hit him in the ear. "You hear me now? MY time."

A monitor in the RV showed the view of the transmitting cameras hidden on Rico's SUV. The team heard someone talking near it then the driver's side door opened and a man leaned in and popped the hood. They saw Cruz lift the hood. "What the hell's he doing?" Tanaka asked.

They heard Cruz working under the hood then their surveillance equipment stopped transmitting. "Shit, son-of-a-bitch took the battery," said Morrison.

"We still have Rico's pin until he gets out of range," said Jamieson. "Same thing with the earpieces."

"I'll send out the drone," said George who flipped a switch.

The monitor then showed that Naldo was escorting Rico to another building. A banger ran up to Naldo and whispered something to him. Naldo turned to Rico. "You fucked up my business for the last time, Councilman." Naldo swiveled his body toward one of his men, "Lock him up!"

"Wait. We have to talk." Naldo's men grabbed Rico who struggled against their hold as they hustled him away. In the chaos, the American flag pin cam on Rico's collar, shook loose and tumbled to the ground then disappeared beneath the shuffle of feet and dust.

Night had fallen, marking the next phase of team ShowGun's operation. George's drone sent back images of tiny lights flickering amid the rubble and collapsed buildings. George glanced over to Rico's pin cam feed monitor which was now dark.

He muttered a curse and moved on to the next task, expertly operating the joystick to the drone's night-vision camera. On the monitor, he saw that the three teams — Morrison's, Jamieson's and Tanaka's — were at their positions just outside the Alamo.

Mair and Wilson were prone with their sniper rifles at their designated spot overlooking the target when they heard George report, "I've got eyes on the teams. Bad news, we lost Rico's pin cam." They acknowledged by clicking twice on their transmitters.

From just outside the Alamo's front gates, Tanaka scanned the area with night-vision binoculars. He had a traditional Japanese short sword, a tantō, in a sheath behind him. His two Marines stood by with one of them carrying a rope and grappling hook.

George watched the drone monitor. Morrison's and Jamieson's teams used their grappling hooks to scale the walls and enter the Alamo from other positions. "Team one and two are going in," George reported into his transmitter.

From their sniper position, Wilson panned his rifle. Through his night scope, he picked up Morrison's and Jamieson's teams as they moved further in. Mair did the same. Her night scope revealed Tanaka and his two Marines appear atop the front gate wall then disappear over it.

Meanwhile, three armed bangers slowly made their way single-file along a ridge, their routine patrol taking them closer to Tanaka's position. Suddenly, a bullet struck the trailing banger and he tumbled to the ground.

Mair artfully worked the bolt of her rifle, quickly loading another round into the chamber.

The second banger, unaware of his comrade's fate, turned around at the sound of the thud and shushed him, only to be met with another bullet a split second later.

Wilson calmly loaded another round into his own rifle.

Uneasy, the final banger turned around and saw his dead buddies. His eyes scanned the landscape frantically before he was also struck by a bullet, collapsing onto the ground just feet away from Tanaka's team. Tanaka and his men looked to the top of the ridge and spotted the other two bodies. One of the Marines flashed a "Thumbs up" to Mair and Wilson who exchanged satisfied smiles before Mair chambered another round.

At the transportation area, Morrison and his men helped Schizwicki skillfully place explosives at strategic points around the gas pump, fuel trucks, and large tanks. Sweat dripped down their brows as they worked quickly and efficiently, keenly aware of the danger that surrounded them. Morrison's voice crackled through his transmitter as he relayed their progress: "Just a few more to go. We should be able to rendezvous at section D right on schedule." The only response was two faint clicks through his earpiece, signaling everyone's understanding. Suddenly, a rumbling engine sounded in the distance, and a truck loaded with bangers screeched into view. Morrison's team swiftly ducked behind cover, ready for whatever would ensue.

At the arsenal, there were two flashes of silent gun fire. The two guards stationed at the doors collapsed to the ground, dead. Without hesitation, Jamieson, Bobby and their team rushed up to the doors. "Jamieson, you still on schedule?" Morrison's strained voice came over Jamieson's transmitter. Jamieson double-clicked to confirm, then his team dragged the bodies inside and closed the doors behind them. In the dark interior, everyone turned on their vest flashlights. Jamieson quickly surveyed the area before directing Bobby to a specific spot. Working efficiently, they all began planting explosives in strategic locations.

Inside the Latino Camp, the air was thick with the scent of hairspray and acetone as the women huddled together fixing their hair, reapplying overdone makeup, and repairing the chips in their elaborately painted nails. The men lounged around their various stashes of belongings, drinking and fiddling with their weapons. Each group had its nightly traditions.

In the flickering light of the campfire, a shirtless beefcake guy began a striptease, much to the delight of the women who were cheering him on. With each undulation of his pelvis, he unzipped his fly and pulled out a large cucumber, causing the girls to roar in laughter. He playfully tossed it to one of them before continuing his performance.

Suddenly, the scrawny Rooster burst into the camp, accidentally crashing into Beefcake who immediately shouted "Faggot."

"Eat shit and die," Rooster fired back as Beefcake spat at him.

The two began to fight, but before it could escalate further, Big Frankie appeared and announced, "There's action in the arena in ten minutes." Addressing Rooster, he added, "Naldo wants a full house." Beefcake and Rooster instantly separated and the camp emptied as everyone made their way towards the arena.

Rooster continued on to the Blacks Camp shouting, "Hey, Bros and Hoes. Arena. Ten minutes." The Black leader, who was flipping through Hustler magazine, got up nonchalantly, his sweaty, bare, scarred-up chest glistening in the firelight. The other gang members rushed out of their building. Rooster left and ran through various debris to the next camp.

At the Asian Camp, Rooster greeted them with an over-the-top declaration: "Kon'nichiwa, bitches and motherfuckers... arena time! Sayonara, lantern heads." Koji, the Asian leader, in his 20s, tall and heavily tattooed, threw a piece of fruit that smacked Rooster in the back of the head as he hightailed it out of there.

Rooster then rushed in and brazenly grabbed a beer off a table at the Whites Camp. "Guten nacht, knockwursts. Arena. Be there." He gave the Nazi salute as he ran out shouting, "Sieg Heil!"

Back at the transportation area, the air was thick with the smell of gasoline as Morrison and Schizwicki were still stalled at their position. A group of bangers, their vehicle idling nearby, were unloading gas cans and filling them up with fuel.

Simultaneously, Tanaka and his team made their way between two buildings. As they passed a doorway, four bangers stumbled out, clearly caught off guard. With quick precision, Tanaka's team eliminated all but one of the bangers. Tanaka himself took down the last one, using a chokehold to subdue him before demanding, "Where do you lock people up?" The banger struggled, grabbed Tanaka's arm and tried to pull it away from choking him but only succeeded in having a chunk of skin sliced away by Tanaka's waiting knife. Tanaka then muffled the banger's screams with his hand, leaving the man no choice but to point in the direction of the lock up. Grateful for the information, Tanaka thanked him by swiftly cutting his throat then the Marines promptly dragged the bodies back into the building.

Tanaka's team positioned themselves across from a door with "JAIL" scrawled above it. Five guards stood watch — three on the roof and two at the door. It took mere moments for Tanaka to appear atop the roof, his throwing spikes taking out two guards while his short sword dispatched the third. On the ground, each Marine quickly eliminated a door guard with precise shots. One guard managed to survive but before he could call for help, Tanaka jumped down from the roof and landed on his windpipe, crushing it under his weight.

With no time to waste, Tanaka and his men swiftly moved to the jail door, one Marine retrieving the keys from a dead guard and silently unlocking it. The team rushed in, weapons at the ready, but they were met with a surprising sight — the jail was occupied by only a handful of lowlifes and no sign of Rico. Tanaka scanned the empty cells, jaw set, recalculating. Then a burst of static filled their earpieces, drowning out the sounds of their surroundings. They strained to hear the voices that followed, one of them belonging to Rico. In the distance, they could make out the faint roar of a crowd. The men quickly exited and locked the door behind them, ready to continue their search for Rico.

Naldo's voice came through next, tauntingly saying, "Mr. Councilman doesn't look so important now, does he?" The cheers of the crowd swelled and then gave way to more static before complete silence fell.

Tanaka tapped his earpiece in frustration and glanced at his teammates, who all shook their heads in confusion. They removed their earpieces and strained to pinpoint the source of the commotion. One of the Marines pointed eagerly to a location on their far right.

Carefully and quietly, the team moved towards their designated spot and soon found themselves across from a large arena. They scanned their surroundings for any signs of danger or movement. "Our friend needs to go home," reported Tanaka. "He's at D-three. Are we ready to exfil?"

Jamieson's voice crackled over their earpieces. "Affirmative."

Then Morrison's. "We got a delay. Gimme five."

The atmosphere was tense and chaotic at the transportation area where Morrison, Schizwicki, and their team were still blocked. The sounds of cheers echoed from the nearby arena, causing tension to rise even more for the already anxious bangers.

"We're out of time," Schizwicki exclaimed with urgency, prompting the team to move in.

The bangers, caught off guard, scrambled to defend themselves against the relentless Marines who engaged them in ferocious hand-to-hand combat. Schizwicki, a crazed dynamo, used his strength and agility to bounce bangers off tanks like ragdolls, before tossing them into the waiting arms of his fellow Marines who swiftly snapped their necks. In one final act of defiance, a lone banger managed to slice Schizwicki's arm before being met with a fatal blow as Schizwicki thrust his knife under the guy's armpit and yanked downward.

With all the bangers now dead, Morrison turned to check on Schizwicki, asking "You okay?"

"Yeah. I'll finish up," replied Schizwicki, determination etched in his tone.

Morrison then gestured to one of the Marines and ordered him to tend to Schizwicki's injury. The Marine grabbed his med kit and quickly wrapped Schizwicki's arm as the rest of the team left to complete their mission. In a show of solidarity, Morrison and Schizwicki worked together to set more explosives before finally making their escape.

The arena was actually a cleared out space amid the rubble and downed buildings of the Alamo. Near the center, there was a pole with a steel ring attached to the top with a rope threaded through the ring. One end of the rope dangled down with a thick noose, while the other was tightly gripped in the hands of Big Frankie. Blocks of concrete served as bleachers filled with dozens of bangers, laughing, chatting with each other and playing games on their phones. Obviously not their first execution. The other gang leaders sat down front waiting for the promised spectacle.

Naldo and Cruz shoved Rico into the arena, his body already bruised and battered, his hands tightly bound behind his back. Cruz eagerly slipped the noose over his head, tightening it around his neck with a sadistic grin.

"How about a little enthusiasm?" Naldo shouted to the crowd.

Too busy with their own shit, not many responded at first so Naldo went bigger, "WAKE THE FUCK UP!"

The crowd now took Naldo's order seriously and erupted with shouts of, "Tune him up." and "Fuck him up."

The noose dug deeply into Rico's neck, making it difficult for him to speak. Despite the pain and fear, he managed to choke out a few words. "I just wanted to say..." His voice trailed off as he knew any words would be futile in this brutal game of life or death.

Naldo cocked his ear, straining to hear over the loud jeers and taunts of the crowd. "What's that?" he asked, his voice barely audible above the noise. "We can't hear you, Mr. Big Shit. You trying to say something? Speak up."

Rico's chest heaved as he struggled to take in enough oxygen amidst the tight noose. The crowd continued to boo and curse at him, their faces twisted with hate.

"Shut up!" Naldo bellowed, bringing the noisy crowd to a sudden silence. He motioned for Cruz to loosen the noose, giving Rico a chance to speak again.

"We may disagree on many things," Rico gasped, his throat raw from the pressure from the rope, "but the killing of innocent women and children? Let's set up talks on neutral ground and…"

"You don't get it, do you?" Naldo sneered. "You're not here to negotiate."

Rico knew he had nothing left to lose at this point. With a last burst of defiance, he spat out one final insult. "Coward."

"What did you say?" Naldo growled dangerously, his facade of control starting to crumble. He stepped closer with a menacing glare.

"I said you fucking COWARD!" The words were spat out with venom, Rico's face twisted into a sneer.

The crowd perked up at the sudden tension in the air, sensing that something was about to happen. "Oooooohhhh… Oh, shit!" someone whispered as they all leaned forward in their seats.

"You're nothing but a stupid, low-life punk," Rico continued, his voice rising with each word. Naldo stood his ground but his body was tensing to the point of breaking. He took one step forward and walloped Rico in the gut. The councilman laughed through the pain and shouted to the crowd, "This is your leader? Look at him. See how scared he is of me."

Naldo looked out at the crowd and saw a mixture of smirks and blank stares directed toward him. Anger surged through him and he tore the noose off of Rico, cutting his hands free before shoving him roughly to the ground along with giving him a solid kick. Naldo then stuck his knife into the pole. "Let's see who's the pussy now," he snarled.

But before he could make another move, Rico charged at him like a bull. The two men engaged in a brutal and bloody fight that lasted for several minutes, both on the ground and on their feet. Despite his age and condition, Rico was holding his own against Naldo until a well-placed kick to the ribs sent him crashing to the ground with a sickening CRACK! The crowd roared with excitement and encouragement for Naldo to finish him.

Naldo walked over to retrieve his knife from the pole. As he turned back towards Rico, ready to deliver the final blow, smoke canisters suddenly rained down from above and filled the arena with a thick cloud of smoke. The fight came to an abrupt halt as both men struggled to see through the haze and for Naldo to make sense of what was happening.

The two teams, led by Jamieson and Morrison, moved in. Schizwicki's bandage was drenched in blood. All hell broke loose as the bangers scattered and began shooting wildly. Rico searched for Naldo but he had disappeared in the smoke.

Tanaka and his squad of Marines quickly moved in to rescue Rico who was badly injured. Despite the pain, Rico remained determined as he urged them towards a specific direction. "There's something we have to get," said Rico. "This way." Both Marines supported Rico as they moved out.

Tanaka spoke into his transmitter, "We have Rico."

Rico led them confidently towards the Communications Center, with Morrison and his men providing cover fire.

As they reached the entrance, they were met by Koji, the fierce Asian leader, making a hasty escape with three of his bangers. The two sides took cover and engaged in a heated exchange of bullets. The Marines showed no mercy as they swiftly eliminated Koji's followers. But Koji himself was not going down without a fight. He ran out of ammo and turned to flee, only to find himself boxed in.

"Protect Rico. I got this one," said Tanaka as he moved toward Koji with his sword drawn. In a desperate attempt to survive, Koji drew his knife and prepared to face off against Tanaka. But Tanaka seemed to relish his new opponent's bravado. He calmly sheathed his sword and unsheathed his own knife.

With a lone Marine by his side, Rico cautiously stepped into the dimly lit Communications Center. The other Marine positioned himself outside the door, ready for any potential threats. Suddenly, two deafening explosions rocked the room, plunging it into darkness and filling the air with choking dust. Rico stumbled blindly around in search of the backup drive, his heart pounding in his chest. Finally, a small emergency light flickered on. His Marine was on the ground, Big Frankie hammering him with heavy blows. The Marine took the punishment, got a knee up between them and forced some space.

Before Rico could react, Naldo appeared out of nowhere and tackled Rico to the ground, his hands closing in on his throat. Struggling for breath and grasping at anything within reach, Rico finally found a computer cord and looped it over Naldo's head. With every ounce of strength he had left, he pulled on the cord until Naldo lay motionless on top of him.

BANG-BANG! Two gunshots rang out. The Marine, with gun in hand, pushed himself up off the ground, fired another two rounds then stepped over Big Frankie's lifeless body to help Rico to his feet as he secured the precious backup drive.

The fierce sparring between Tanaka and Koji spilled over to the side of the building, their swift movements creating a blur of hands and knives. Meanwhile, the Marine stationed at the doorway relentlessly engaged with more bangers, his gun firing off three-round bursts. Suddenly, he caught sight of Rico approaching and took a hit from one of the bangers to his bulletproof vest before returning fire. With precise aim, he took down the last banger just as he himself was struck in the head.

As Rico and the other Marine emerged from the building, they passed the fallen soldier lying motionless on the ground. The Marine paused for just a moment, meeting the dead soldier's eyes before moving forward as Rico claimed his weapon.

They turned the corner and saw Tanaka still locked in a fierce battle with Koji who had his back to them. Rico's gun was raised and aimed at Koji, ready to fire at any moment.

Tanaka shouted, "No!"

"We're out of time!" Rico called out.

Suddenly, the transportation area erupted — fuel trucks, storage tanks and the gas pump all going up at once — the force of it rocking the ground beneath them and causing Tanaka, who had been standing on a pile of rubble, to lose his footing. With lightning reflexes, Koji charged at Tanaka for the kill. But Tanaka used the force of his fall to roll under Koji, deftly sweeping his legs out from under him. As Koji crashed to the ground, Tanaka swiftly sliced his throat with a clean cut.

Back at the arena, Morrison saw the bangers on the far left and right then yelled to Jamieson, "They're trying to outflank us. Pull back."

Outside the Communications Center, Tanaka and Rico's Marine heard Morrison's warning over their earpieces. They joined the other teams as they pulled back from the arena. Rico did his best to keep up and stay out of harm's way at the same time.

As the teams fell back, they took fire, even from above. Morrison shouted into his transmitter, "Fire-team, engage. We're taking fire from high ground." Three of Morrison's snipers rose out of the rubble and picked off the bangers on rooftops.

Out of nowhere, Rooster, on a zip line and wielding a huge knife, came flying down at Morrison. Jamieson spotted Rooster and blew him out of the air with his shotgun. Rooster landed at Morrison's feet, his orange hair now tinted bright red. Morrison flashed Jamieson a smile an instant before — BAM-BAM-BAM! Morrison was hit multiple times. He slumped to his knees. Jamieson whipped his gun on the shooters. Took them out in a barrage of shots. He then pulled Morrison to his feet. The team returned fire as they moved through the Alamo while the snipers helped lay down cover.

The teams and snipers ran, pursued by bangers all the way. They passed a building marked "Drug Store." When they cleared it, Morrison signaled the snipers who took cover, fired, and held back the bangers. Schizwicki remote-detonated his explosives. BOOM! The Drug Store blew to high heaven and was aglow in flaming sunset colors. Bangers were hurled sky high while some others skirted the flames.

Snipers followed the teams now coming upon the arsenal. Morrison again signaled his men. They took cover and fired.

As Bobby sprinted through the debris, he caught sight of two bangers, their guns raised and ready to fire on Schizwicki. With lightning-fast reflexes, he pushed his partner out of the way just as the first shots rang out. Pain seared through his side and leg as bullets impacted his body, but he remained determined to protect Schizwicki at all costs.

Schizwicki triggered the detonator just as Bobby collapsed to the ground with a groan. BOOM! Massive black and orange balls of fire rocketed into the sky while thick clouds of smoke billowed up in their wake. The deafening sound of multiple RPGs being launched filled the air, adding to the chaotic scene before them. Schizwicki threw Bobby over his shoulder and handed off his P90 machine gun to Rico who, despite great pain, helped lay down cover as the teams were close to exiting the Alamo. Schizwicki then blew the front gate.

High above the Alamo, Mair and Wilson feverishly fired on bangers. "I can't keep up," she shouted. Then she remembered something. "Oh shit!" she exclaimed, rushing back to their vehicles.

A few moments later, Wilson felt a vehicle pull up behind him. He turned and saw Mair backing up a truck. He continued to fire as Mair ran to the back of the truck, quickly opening a wooden crate and pulling a lever. The sides of the crate fell away, revealing a gatling gun.

Wilson wasted no time. He jumped in as Mair set the sights for distance. He then took position to feed the ammo. "It's all yours," he said.

Mair took her place behind the powerful weapon. With her finger on the trigger, BAAARAAKKKKK! she unleashed a barrage of deadly full metal jacket fury. As the teams made their escape through the front gate of the Alamo, Mair mowed down countless bangers who attempted to follow them.

Schizwicki shouted, "Hit the dirt!" Everyone dove for cover behind mounds of rubble as more bangers exited after them. Instantly, Schizwicki detonated another set of explosives that sent chunks of concrete and steel girders flying down onto the trailing bangers, entombing them and sealing off the entrance.

Debris fell near the teams and a chunk of concrete bashed Jamieson in the back. Razor wire broke loose, uncoiled, then shot across a large swath of bangers trying to escape along the perimeter. It sliced into them as if carving up turkeys and 'punk-in' pies.

The compound was rocked by massive explosions that erupted from within its walls. From a bird's-eye view captured by the drone, the Alamo appeared as nothing but a ball of billowing smoke and fire, growing hotter and brighter with each passing moment.

Later, aerial and ground shots revealed the extent of the destruction, until finally... a news reporter's voiceover accompanied spectacular footage of the aftermath. "These are the scenes last night of what is believed to be a major gang hideout. Police and Fire crews are continuing to investigate the source of the explosions that were heard up to thirty miles away. Initial reports are that multiple large gas storage tanks were somehow ignited. The number of dead, if any, is unknown at this time."

Watching the news footage from their hospital beds were Bobby (shot), Schizwicki (knifed), Morrison (broken ribs from hits on vest), Rico (heavily bruised, broken ribs, and cuts), and Jamieson (bruised back and a broken ankle). Tanaka, uninjured, stood at the doorway watching over them as Mair went around fussing and propping pillows for each patient.

George wheeled himself into the doorway. "We're going to be late," he declared.

Mair looked around at the group before turning back to Rico. "And you were worried about me!" she exclaimed with a mix of teasing and relief. "Now, I'm off to work. See you all soon." George spun his wheelchair around and the two of them left for their new ShowGun gig. George handling weapons; Mair stuntwoman extraordinaire.

A week later at a neighborhood park, a festive crowd gathered while a live band played. In attendance were Mair, Morrison, Jamieson, Bobby, Tanaka, Schizwicki, and others — all in various stages of recovery but determined to celebrate their survival. Two kids chased each other past the group, laughing. Mair watched them go with a smile. When she turned back, Bobby was already looking toward the park entrance where Councilwoman Park was strolling towards them. "He'll come," Mair said. "He just needs a minute with her first."

Meanwhile, Rico stood at Dolores' grave with his head bowed in prayer. A single white rose, symbolizing his enduring love, adorned the top of her gravestone. After saying his goodbyes, he turned and walked away.

As he drove towards the park for the celebration, Dolores' music box played on the dashboard. The lower part of his car was now emblazoned with the words *Javier Rico for Mayor*, a testament to his newfound purpose and determination to honor Dolores' memory by making a positive impact in their community.

THE END

AUTHORS

J Bartell, M.A., is an author, screenwriter, and behavior specialist, renowned for developing and teaching his process known as 'Left-Right Brain Suggestibility.' He was previously a licensed Marriage, Family, and Child Counselor in California. In his mid-thirties, J became Chief of Staff at one of the world's largest therapeutic/educational institutes. At that time, he gave lectures and live demonstrations of Pain, Bleeding, and Muscle Control at UCLA and other venues. His clients included people from all walks of life, but it was his worldwide travels on behalf of affluent, private individuals, including heads-of-state, that put him on the radar of the CIA. For more information about J, visit his website at http://jbartell.com.

Ginger Marin is an actor, author, screenwriter, environmentalist and animal rights advocate. As a former network TV Journalist at NBC News NY, Ginger served as producer and writer for the network's top news shows and various special reports. Ginger is also the author of "Monster on Mars" and "Adventures in Avalon: An Offbeat & Quirky Adult Bedtime Story". To learn more about Ginger's acting and film projects, visit her IMDB page http://www.imdb.me/gingermarin or her personal website https://gingermarin.com. If you want to read how she bemoans the world, check out her blog at http://bioniclady.com